FORWARD

MASTHEAD

Megan Giddings
Anthology Editor

Bix Gabriel
Community Outreach Facilitator

Paul Asta
Book Designer

Mary Elizabeth Watson
Book Design Editor

Readers
Megan Giddings
Josh Denslow
Aubrey Hirsch
L.N. Holmes
Melody Steiner

Proofreaders
Scott Fenton
Melody Steiner
Jennifer Wortman

ISBN: 978-1-941143-12-4

Copyright 2019, Aforementioned Productions.
Rights for individual works published in this volume are held by their creators, except where mentioned below.

Aforementioned colophon is a trademark of Aforementioned Productions.

All rights reserved. No part of this publication may be used or reproduced in any manner whatsoever without written permission, except in the case of brief quotations embodied in critical articles or reviews.

Excerpts from *Action Comics* #400 (1971), *Superman* #338 (1979), and Superman are trademarks and copyright of DC Comics.

Cover illustration by Anuj Shrestha. Jacket designed by Jon Cameron.

Printed in the United States of America. March 2019.

FORWARD

21st CENTURY FLASH FICTION

Edited by
MEGAN GIDDINGS

A|P

CONTENTS

MEGAN GIDDINGS | Editor's Note	1
CHRISTOPHER GONZALEZ | Here's the Situation	9
C. PAM ZHANG | Collection	15
TYRESE COLEMAN | They Reminisce Over You	20
REEM ABU-BAKER | True Stories	25
SJ SINDU | Yellow School Buses	29
DESIREE COOPER | The Choice	33
THIRII MYO KYAW MYINT | Ghost Story	37
ALVIN PARK | Dobson Unit	40
AMINA GAUTIER | Before	43
MONTERICA SADE NEIL | Craving Sugar	48
ANNA CABE | See Me	53
MADHVI RAMANI | Wolf	57

ESHANI SURYA | Between Colitis Flares, Expect the Following Symptoms — 62

MARLIN M. JENKINS | This House Is Our Burned Bodies — 65

GEORGE ABRAHAM | origin story, to be written on the walls of my childhood home in blood — 69

RUTH JOFFRE | A Girl Turns to Stone — 72

MARÍA ISABEL ÁLVAREZ | Peña Blanca, Guatemala — 74

YALIE KAMARA | Mirror — 79

ERICA FREDERICK | I Want So Much from This Life — 83

GENE KWAK | No Frills — 86

PATRIZ BILIRAN | Secrets in Our Cigarettes — 90

URSULA VILLARREAL-MOURA | The Equivalent of _____ — 93

DENNIS NORRIS II | Daddy's Boy — 96

KRISTINE ONG MUSLIM | Holocene: Microfilm Reel 82 — 99

YUN WEI | How to Catch a Sun — 103

MAGGIE SU | Circumnavigation — 107

W. TODD KANEKO | Planets in Miniature: On Kandor and Compression in Flash Fiction	115
ALICITA RODRÍGUEZ | Focus on Flash Fiction	121
MARCOS GONSALEZ | On the Short Form	126
ALLISON NOELLE CONNER | The Sentence Turns Back: Jamaica Kincaid's "Girl"	131
EDITORS' ROUNDTABLE | Tara Campbell, Leland Cheuk, Tyrese Coleman, Bix Gabriel	137
CONTRIBUTORS	151

EDITOR'S NOTE

Once upon a time, I wrote a flash story. I edited and proofread and researched all the places that "might be a good fit." I revised and edited again to make my sentences clear, to make sure that even though time was compressed, a reader wouldn't get confused. I sent the story out. And I waited. I started a new story. I waited. And eventually, I found out that the story was going to be published. And it was such good news. I told my husband and friends and teachers. Emojis were used. I did the proofreading, discussed things seriously with an editor. And my heart felt so good to have someone taking my work seriously enough that they fussed over the order of the words, wanted to talk semi-colon versus em dash.

And finally, the issue was live. And I was very happy, but something kept pulling at me. And this situation has happened so many times before. Sometimes, I realize what's going on fairly quickly because the magazine is an online journal that uses author photos. Sometimes, it takes seeing all the contributors tagged on social media. There are many ways where it becomes clear, but then it's unavoidable: I am the only person in the issue who is a person of color.

And sometimes, I would take a deep breath and think, this is how publishing is. And the only way to fix it is to stay involved and keep going. And sometimes, I would write an email to the very nice editor encouraging them to solicit and seek out more writers of color or even saying these people would be a great fit for your magazine. And sometimes—and I know many of you have been here—I've started to question my work and who it's for.

I've become a wise enough writer and person to know that there's no such thing as universality in writing. On a basic level, to use a cliché: one person's trash is another person's treasure. Etc. At the same time, historically, universality in the United States means whiteness. You can, if you're willing to acknowledge how cultural institutions affect language and art, trace this back in part to the United States' 1850 Census. At that time, you only had to choose a race if you weren't white. If you were white, you were a man or a woman. And that reverberates still in how writers, at least in the US, often approach character and description in fiction.

So, it becomes a spiral. Am I writing the best work I can? Or am I writing for an audience that implicitly excludes myself, my family, my friends? And why do I have to think about things like authenticity and who I am writing for? Wouldn't the punk rock thing be to just do whatever I want and who cares? And beneath all those questions is loneliness. I want to feel like my work is important. Not just something that makes the editors look good, but is so urgent and beautiful and engaging, they had to respond. That I am speaking to humanity and living, not filling a quota. I am a person.

The point of this anthology for me isn't to demonstrate the best of flash fiction. I'm not really a person who believes in bests. The point is to show off the many ways a very short story can be written. It's to show that there are many different writers out there engaging with the incredible elasticity of flash fiction. I think flash is going to continue to grow in popularity because it's one of the few areas in fiction that forces constraint and thus comes the play that can come from following the rules. A writer and reader of flash builds new thought-muscles, finds new ways to play. I think many readers and writer-readers are going to leave this anthology inspired to try new forms and think about how to push their own writing or even their definitions of what a story can be.

One of the magic things about books is the kinship that

EDITOR'S NOTE

comes from reading something you like or love. A story that keeps you up all night or makes you re-read it three times in a row because you don't want to leave that land, that language, those people. And I hope by pulling this collection together—and hopefully we'll get to do more editions of this that feature different people from different places—that for the writers in this anthology and especially for aspiring writers and even for me, that we'll all feel a little less alone. I hope that this tiny book I helped build—and thank you again everyone who has contributed time and money and skills to this—gives us all a new home.

This anthology is also a conversation. There are stories in here that are about racism and violence and moving to different countries and considerations of race and an exploration of what it means to be in places where you're not a default person, you're a _____ person. And there are stories in here about liars and sex and djinn and very unusual spiders. We write in the third-person past-tense, close about families. We write in the distant language of medical questionnaires. We write in first-person plural. We write for ourselves and we write for each other and we write for you.

Megan Giddings
Anthology Editor

STORIES

HERE'S THE SITUATION
Christopher Gonzalez

There's a guy, Danny, sitting on our stoop. He's got his face in his hands and he's tapping his left foot, slapping the heel against our bottom step, counting down the seconds until he loses his shit.

He's waiting for Eduardo. Like all the others.

Here's how it started:
In high school, Eduardo picked up a new guy every few weeks in the spring, every couple of days in the summer. He let his dick rest through the winter. Sometimes I tagged along on the dates—I'd sit on a bench in the park, staring out at the little creek while they sucked each other off behind a group of trees. I never participated or anything freaky like that, not that Eduardo ever invited me to join. But he

needed to keep me close. For all the good times, he said, but especially the bad.

Here's the situation:
Danny has always greeted me with a smile, toothy beyond what I deserve. When his late nights with Eduardo started folding into Saturday morning breakfasts, I set my alarm to wake hours before either of them would stumble out of Eduardo's room. I whipped up tall stacks of blueberry pancakes twelve weekends in a row; the three of us sipped café con leche at the kitchen table, our forks dripping with syrup, our feet bare, and hair messy. I lost full days to the haze of those slow mornings, each one stretching out like a long, delicious nap.

Here's how it often plays out:
I go up to the guy and sputter out any name, say, "Andrew?" (This is not strategic at all on my part. I rarely get their names.) The guy then cocks his head up at me like I am trying to start a fight. "Helios," he might correct me. Coldly, that's how he'd do it. I then tell Helios-Andrew-Sergio-whatever that our friend Eduardo won't be back anytime soon. I might toss in a detail about a month-long vacation, a family emergency, his mother found dead on the side of a street, his brother taking a bullet in the back, a blood

transfusion needed that only Eduardo could fulfill, and that in light of these events, instead of occupying space outside my apartment, it would be best for the man to go.

The good ones, the guys for whom I feel the most, do leave. They take the hint and disappear.

Here's the situation:
Danny, wearing Eduardo's college hoodie, leaning against his door, waiting for him to finish up with a work call.

Or Danny, curled up with a book at the end of our sofa, the early morning sun dissecting him through the blinds.

Or Danny, alone at our kitchen table, half past 2am, a bottle of blueberry wine drained; he sits in silence, chin in hand.

Here's what I've learned:
There is power in ending a relationship. Even the ones that were never yours.

Here's how it can go bad:
They sit for too long, faces cupped in hands, the sun sinking down on us. They get indignant. Say something like "He can't just do me like this," or "Nobody has the balls to break it off in person anymore?" or "Who the fuck are

you?" or "No, really, who the fuck are you?" or "Then why are you so fucking smiley about it." They often scan my face for permission to scream or run away, but I never stay long enough to see what they decide. This is for the best. I squeeze past them, wedge myself between their slumped body and the stoop railing, through the door and straight into my apartment, where I start a pot of coffee and wait, in the darkness, for Eduardo to come home.

Here's what I remember:
Our classmates fawning over Eduardo. And why wouldn't they? He could roll his Rs better than anyone. When he danced bachata and merengue in the school gym, he moved across the floor as if it had been waxed just for his feet; I was good for a dance, maybe two, if my partner didn't mind my taking a breather every couple of songs, and I spoke both English and Spanish with a lisp-y tongue, the words coming out wet and scrambled.

Here's the worst it's gone:
Helios-Andrew-Sergio-whatever got into the apartment. I had been preparing dinner, a stew bulked up with potatoes and carrots. The chef's knife was on the kitchen table. I imagined him getting there first, holding the blade against my throat. But I was quicker: I blinked and saw the flash of

red—how easily the blade passed through his stomach, like popping a water balloon, all the tension breaking away.

Here's how the last guy left it:
"He'll never love you."

Here's the situation:
Danny raises his head from his lap. He says, "Eduardo isn't returning any of my calls, Mateo. Do you know what's up?" I consider a pre-packaged reply, or backing away and running around the corner. I could lie and lie and lie again.

Here's how I sleep:

Here's the situation:
Danny is sitting on our stoop. His frown could draw blood.

Here's what I miss:
When we were kids, I would strap on a pair of retro roller skates and Eduardo would let me tether myself to his bike. I weaved over asphalt and brick-paved roads behind him. While we sped through the city, the air scraping against my

face, I felt like a kite not quite catching the wind, thinking that if he could go just for a little longer and if I tightened my grip, I might take flight.

Here's the situation:
I will hand Danny a bag of groceries, invite him inside. I'll slice open a loaf of bread, slather its fluffy interior with butter, toast it, and serve it alongside strong Bustelo. We'll sit together at the table, Danny and me, and hold each other in place until Eduardo walks in through the door. Then, together, we'll let go.

COLLECTION

C. Pam Zhang

This variety of spider is born dead, Noll told us. Stiff packets of chitin and darkness. Teensy tiny organs rattling like dried beans if we listened with the right tools (which Noll had). Out-of-state scientist came with his white van and silver knives to explain to us what our forest held. Only when someone warmed these spiders, he said, provided a violent friction from the mashing of flesh (like their mommies) or the point of a needle (like Noll) did they wriggle to life.

★

Noll asked could he pick us up at midnight and we said, *Okay.* Yawning as if our maiden chests didn't hum under threadbare dresses. *Okay. Whenever.* Midnight was when the spiders grew active and stirred from spider dreams. We lapsed into dreams of our own while waiting, tangled into a many-legged organism of sisterhood breathing one sticky breath. Our lids grew heavy. We rubbed gunk from our lashes that crumbled like tiny eggs.

The world flared red light and a thousand legs danced in the veins of our shut eyes. Noll's van came swinging up the drive. *Aw shit*, we said, shielding our faces. *Cut your lights*. His sweaty hands helped us in. We sucked the sweets he fed us and grew heavy, stretched out to sleep across the plastic tubs he laid down in the back. Each one just long enough for each of us. Felt him touch us then like a husband in the dark, his knife parting our clothes. We smiled at the tickle. Two hours later, woke up as Noll poured our clacking bones into the forest.

★

We went along because he'd asked so nice. A pretty blue fire he built us, that night he proposed our forest trip. *I want to know what's in there*, he teased as he tapped our heads, and we giggled.

Used to be that marriageable girls went collecting for wedding trousseaus in these parts. When these were mountains instead of nubs, when there were husbands to be had. When we had tongues we rolled the word around: *Trousseau*. Imagining ancestral mothers and aunts garlanded with flowers, animal pelts scribbled on their nether sides with ropy veins. *Strictly superstition*, frowned the scientists. *Now open wide and say AH!* Same way they always spoke of the centuries before they kept a record, before their cameras bobbed along our misty roads and stood beside our sag-mouthed scarecrows. Hoping to spy the secret of our long mountain lives. We chain-smoked, stared into the blinking red eyes. *Inconclusive*, the scientists sighed and back they went. Except for Noll. He stayed. Different, him. A hunger to prod and rip and taste whatever we showed. He even ate possum, tearing the meat bare-handed with no mind for its bloody drips. Fixing us all the while with his pretty green eyes.

So we spread our knees at his chemical flame, warming. Eying him sideways and long-lashed, in the manner of deer observing the hunter from behind a blind of trees: hard-horned but shy.

*

Sure enough, we tumbled out the van at the hour of spiders. Lay studying their shiny mandibles, their characteristic bristle pattern. As Noll had instructed. Hours passed, then years, before we remembered to yawn. Time moves funny in our forest. The scientists who siphoned and magnified our blood declared us inbred, deviants, but it wasn't on purpose like they said. How were we to avoid our own great-great-grand-aunts and cousins wandering out of the forest with lace collars flapping on their breasts, a mess of kids raised before realizing: Oops. You'd need keen eyes to tell that style of collar hadn't been seen since eighteen and ninety-two when the machines unhooked our mountain and left it a laceless, coalless scar. Real keen eyes and us half-blind from the acid fog. Anyhow, we implore you to think on what scientists know and don't—they who "discovered" extinct fish swimming cool as you please in our caves. Time moved funny while we lay with the spiders. Trees molted, mold grew, animals died and turned to mush then bog then peat then coal and all of this happened again and again every second. We yawned and remembered our original purpose. *Gone collecting.* By the time we rose, shaking off years of dirt, we'd acquired skeins of spider silk. Egg sacs bumped our ribs like dark jewels. A worthy trousseau.

*

No one had to tell us marriage is the end of the fairy tale. Noll's no prince. We saw his flaws a while back. Under his beard, his weak chin. Under his carpet, bloodstains. Still.

FORWARD

Make a meal of what you got, our mother and great-great-grand-aunt said. She'd managed to raise us before anyone realized she was dead, and even after that she soldiered on, dropping fingerbones into bread dough and clattering advice from her jaw: *That price is a joke. Rain coming heavy this year.* We'd even dug her up to ask about Noll before we went collecting. Her verdict: *Mean but whip-smart. The right girls can make him into something.* We accepted him as work. So when we turned up on Noll's doorstep some years later (walking slow without muscles) and found the green bleached from his eyes, we accepted him, and when he crossed his liverspotted hands and opened his gums to scream, we accepted him, and when he stomped the spiders we'd carried so thoughtfully between our ribs we were a little angry, sure, but we had centuries to learn each other's ways and looking at him we remembered our wedding night in the van, him bearing down in the dark so dear and skinny and hungry, silver tools penetrating us down to joy and bone. The way he peeled off dresses, skins, muscles. Most of all the way he cradled our brains so tenderly in his tubs. Studying us as if we were the precious things. Us! We would have blushed if we could. The spiders' legs went pitter-patter among our ribs. *Hi, honey,* we said.

THEY REMINISCE OVER YOU

Tyrese Coleman

Corbin was shot while listening to Pete Rock and CL Smooth's "T.R.O.Y." He'd entered the bodega on Fourth Street just as the song's jam intro ended. The first mellow riff of the saxophone solo kicked in through his black bubble headphones, and Trina McIver, wearing a concrete-gray puffy-coat that blended in with the city behind her, opened the store glass door. Long dookie braids snatched to the top of her head pulled her eyes into slim cat-like slits or Egyptian Cleopatra eyes, gold door knocker earrings bumped her cheeks, and the music in his ears animated her steps into a summertime breeze, the antithesis of the air outside.

His headphones smelled of the Sportin' Waves gel his uncle got him using—*Bitches love good hair, Jack. Muthafucking Christopher Williams-light-skin-good-hair-having and shit. Learn to sing 'stead of playing with them records and beep bopping. Singers get all the bitches.* This morning, Corbin stood in the bathroom mirror and washed up in the sink. The hot water wasn't working, the kerosene heater flicked and faded. Cold beat him woke when he lifted his shirt and washed his underarms, pulled open his sweats and rubbed Irish Springs on his quivering balls. His breath smoked around him as he pushed air in and out through his teeth to amp up like a boxer readying for a fight. One last breath before he dipped his head in the depths of the freezing water. His fade, a good quarter inch high, needed to be wet for the curls. His mama banged on the door, yelling she had to go work, and get out that bathroom, and when did he spend so much time putting on clothes, must be that girl, and I swear Michael Corbin Francis Junior, you bet not come in this house with no gotdamn babies!

The first sentence of the song was the last sentence he heard before *pop pop* and falling forward. His black bubble headphones stayed put, the music melodious in his dying ears, and if he does die, it would, at least, be while listening to a masterpiece.

The saxophone repeated and mixed with the police sirens. His hand still in his pocket palmed a Panasonic cassette player. Corbin had enough strength to turn the ridged dial up and block out the noise.

The scent of grape soda lip gloss, the sticky softness of her mouth over the right side of his face while the other pressed cold tile, the heaviness of her arm across his back—Trina was there.

The first time he'd suggested they meet at the bodega on Fourth she'd asked, *Who skips school to go to the library?* Sweaty gum had sliced between her teeth before she popped it, and Corbin learned to count her gum snaps: the more she popped, the less her interest. Calculus class: a pop a minute, AP English: silence.

There on the bodega floor, he heard nothing but this song.

She sat next to him in both classes, purple lip gloss, a plastic pencil, and textbook in front of her—not one of those chicks who pretended to be dumb because she thought it was cute.

In the summer, her legs browned the shade of a worn penny.

Skip class to go to the library? she'd asked.

Nah, not the library, the archives, he said, wishing he wore glasses like MC Serch because he was about to drop some knowledge.

Digging through crates, Boo. You'll be my assistant.

He'd been thinking of Trina, the new sample—a doo-wop song with strings and background vocals he wanted to layer in a mix for a local M.C.

FORWARD

Didn't see the three cops pointing their guns or the other black man running down the street and into the bodega. Didn't notice them at all until the man ran into him, pushed him on a shelf, and the shots had already been fired.

A couple months ago, she'd let him in between those thighs. A soft fuzz covered them, and she apologized for not shaving as if he gave a god damn. He felt dumb thinking about Trina and marriage and kids and shit, but the song put it in his head. Or maybe it was her screaming. Or maybe she'd lifted the speakers away from his head, whispered with soft, sticky fluttering lips that wet his earlobe:

"You're going to be a daddy, C."

He let the song soothe him, matched his fading heartbeat to the drum beat overlapping the original sample, an obscure cover by Tom Scott of Jefferson Airplane's "Today." The lyrics to the hippie tune spoke of wanting, knowing what you want, more today than ever.

Someone, one of the cops who shot him, grunted while pushing Trina off Corbin's body. The sudden lightness caused his breath to quicken. He prayed they'd leave his headphones. They were part of his body.

He hoped Trina would hold his mother's hand when they tell her he's gone.

They will wear airbrushed T-shirts to his funeral. Hundreds will attend.

His uncle will sell his mixer and drum machine for too little money.

Trina and his mother will watch old tapes of him rapping in talent shows, talk about how he was going to make it, he would've been a star.

Trina will take their son to the archives, place sweaty bubble speakers over his head, play this song for him, and tell him about his daddy.

An outro of the saxophone riff and an echoing choir wailing like the ghosts, like ancestors still not forgotten, lulled Corbin to rest before the music faded, and the tape rolled *click* to an end.

TRUE STORIES

Reem Abu-Baker

I.

At a dirt-covered park in some Southwestern town, the father and the daughter sit at a plastic picnic table, crinkling bags filled with sliced bread, deli turkey. The scraggly dog lurking around the park makes the father uncomfortable. The father speaks about the dog like the creature is conniving: it's trying to *make* us feed it. The father tosses small pebbles toward the dog, tries to yell it away. The father bristles over many things, the father a man who lives in a world that is hungry, where hunger is a bad thing, everything hungry hunting for the father, hunting for the daughter.

Later, the father does not want the daughter to touch the ocean, but she runs into it anyway, arms flung outward, screaming *water can't hurt me*. Then, of course, she is swept away.

The daughter is not eaten, but she never sees the father again, and that's the history in which she grows older in water and grows fins and washes up on some island where she is filleted and splayed on porcelain.

In the factory farming system, the daughter's body doubles itself, and triples and quadruples and so on, severed pieces reappearing on each plate—wrist, leg, mouth, cunt.

The father is fasting and does not believe in restaurants or islands or cunts, and so really there is no more connection between these two stories, besides the kinds of connections there always are between land and water, between restaurant and fast, between wild dogs and deli meat.

IV.

Frequently, this is a story about languages lost.

The father had a mother who could not speak the right language, and so she did not speak at all. She birthed five children and could not speak their language or the language of anyone in the land where the children were born.

Finally, she birthed the father. The father, freshly birthed, could not speak any languages. The father's mother knew that even though the father did not then speak any languages, he would soon learn to speak the language of the place where he was born, and so she began to imitate every sound the father made. The father's mother gurgled and cooed and screamed like the father, and for a while these were the only sounds the father and the father's mother made.

Slowly, the gurgles sharpened, the coos became words, and the father was saying things like *Mama* and *Baba* and *ana* and *maya*. And so the father's mother also said these words. And they both said more words and more words until they could say many words, until they stacked the words together into sentences and stories.

For a long time, the father's mother could only speak in repetitions of the words of the father. When the father was a teenager, this made him angry. He did not want his mother following him around and repeating all of the words he said and never saying any words of her own.

As an act of rebellion, the father stopped speaking entirely. The father's mother grew sad because the father's silence meant she also had to stop speaking.

A man from the village noticed that the father and the father's mother had both stopped speaking and, being very superstitious, he believed they were possessed by jinn. He approached the father's father to ask if the people in his household were possessed by jinn.

The father's father was so bothered by the idea of the people in his household being possessed by jinn that he opened his mouth to speak, but instead of releasing words, his body sent his voice leaping up from his throat and into the throat of the superstitious man from the village.

The superstitious man from the village now had both his own voice and the father's father's voice. Because he had the voices of two men in the body of one man, the man from the village grew very politically powerful but also very emotionally exhausted, and so he built many wells in the desert and built a city of tunnels at the bottoms of the wells, running through the whole desert. He sent his two voices down opposite tunnels and up through the wells, both the voices speaking about jinn and speaking about the people who'd gone quiet.

The voices would come floating up out of the wells, talking at the villagers as they pulled up buckets of water. This is how the belief in the underground jinn cities at the bottoms of wells came about.

Meanwhile, the father and the father's mother and the father's father were all silent. And then the whole world became silent (except for the voices in the wells), for various specific and personal reasons that don't lend themselves well to generalization, and everyone (except for the voices in the wells) was silent until the end.

YELLOW SCHOOL BUSES
SJ Sindu

In Singapore, halfway through her journey, Nandini sits in a cramped room memorizing her fact sheet. Hot air swirls inside the walls, unmoved by the lethargic, creaking ceiling fan. All five of them have been stacked in here for a week—Nandini, her mother, her three little brothers. Her father had stayed behind in Sri Lanka.

Since leaving their home, her mother cries every night and prays in rapid, never-ending succession. During the days, Nandini's mother sits exhausted against the headboard of the single bed, fanning herself with her own fact sheet. Her brothers nap in a heap, all brown tangled limbs and dirty clothes.

Nandini memorizes her new identity: her name is Preeti Sriranganathan; she is nineteen years old; she wears glasses and lives at 75 Silver Springs Boulevard in Toronto.

"Quick," she says to her mother. "What color are Canadian school buses?"

Her mother glances at the fact sheet she holds in her hand.

"Don't look," Nandini says. "You can't look during the interview."

They've been given explicit instructions to flush the fact sheets down the toilet upon arriving in Toronto, before they reach the customs officers.

Her mother folds up the fact sheet. "When did you get so bossy? You're starting to sound like your father."

Leaving Sri Lanka was her father's doing. Nandini wrote something in her school newspaper, criticizing the gerrymandering by the Sri Lankan government in the latest election. She wrote the piece in a fury the night the election results were announced, and by the next morning the soldiers were at their door, interrupting breakfast with their rifles.

"What color are the school buses in Toronto?"

"Black," her mother says.

Nandini shakes her head.

"White?"

"Yellow, Amma. You need to focus."

There were two soldiers, one dark and mean with a scar running down his cheek. He pressed the barrel of the rifle in her father's face. The other one was shorter, friendlier looking.

Her father begged them to let it go, offered them fancy English whiskey and gold necklaces from her mother's dowry. He showed them papers detailing his appointment as a doctor at a government hospital. They demanded to see Nandini anyway, and she came out shaking from behind her mother's shadow. They pointed their rifles at each of her brothers, asking their ages and whether they were affiliated with the Tigers. After an hour, after drinking her mother's tea and eating the European chocolate her family had gotten as a gift, the soldiers finally left with a bottle of Johnny Walker and her mother's necklace made of real gold coins. Her father took the five of them to the embassy that day, and within a week they were on a plane to Singapore, their life savings depleted.

"Okay, then, smart girl," her mother says, "what color are the uniforms that police officers wear?"

"Blue. Sometimes black."

"What are the petrol stations in Toronto?"

"Petro-Canada," Nandini says. She covers up the fact sheet so she can't cheat. "And…"

"See? I'm not the only one." Her mother leans back and keeps fanning, looking out the lone window at the bustling street outside.

Nandini goes back to reading. Her name is now Preeti. She is nineteen years old. Her father will soon join them in Canada, and then none of them will have to worry about air raids or white van abductions or soldiers with guns. Nandini will get a job, will go to school, will go to college. Her brothers will be fluent in English. Her mother will be happy.

Her name is Preeti. She is nineteen years old. She lives at 75 Silver Springs Boulevard in Toronto. She is innocent; she is still a kid. She is going to live in a safe place, free of worry, a place with clean streets and big shopping malls, where police officers wear blue uniforms and school buses are painted yellow.

THE CHOICE

Desiree Cooper

The moment we read the stick, some of us buckled on the bathroom floor. Having only bled once, we thought it was impossible. Having bled forever, we shook our graying heads and thought, "This is no miracle." Susan, who at fourteen still slept with her favorite doll, bit back the tears and started packing her bags. We knew our mothers would not believe us. Abby bought a ticket to New York to secretly take care of it.

We locked ourselves in the bathroom sobbing while the kids banged on the door: "Mommy, please come out…" Jade tried to convince her live-in girlfriend that she had only gone back to him once.

For some of us, three healthy children were enough. For others, a special needs child was one too many. One day, we would have many children.

One day, decades later, we would still be child free.

The ultrasound technician drew in a deep breath and did not let it out.

Undecided, we waited too long. Decisive, we were instantly clear about what to do. We were happy about it until we weren't.

We borrowed cash from our friends so that it wouldn't show on the insurance bill. We had no insurance. We had insurance, but the D & C was covered only for miscarriages. Brittany's college roommates threw her a "baby shower" with vodka served in sippy cups.

On our knees, we asked God why the rape hadn't been punishment enough. Our aunts said, "You're lucky you won't be butchered in someone's basement like I was."

Lynne was dropped off by her stepfather, along with her suitcase and her cat. We called in sick at the firm even though it was tax season. Mary's boyfriend slapped her and pushed her out of the car. "You better have dinner ready tonight," he said. "And your fat ass better not still be pregnant."

The bus. A cab. The heat. A bike. The snow. The traffic. We were late, but we made it. We were two hours early because we couldn't sit at home alone.

In the waiting room, we would not return a gaze. Our men held us tightly. Jan nervously fiddled with a ring from her make-believe fiancé. We were by ourselves and puffy-faced. Diane was already showing—every time, she seemed to show a few weeks earlier. One couple argued with the receptionist. They had driven from another state, but didn't know about the 24-hour waiting period. Some of us let the tears river while others slumped in pink chairs and listened to our iPods.

We were horrified to be with these people. Full of shame, we fingered a rosary. Full of anger, we cursed God.

"Relax." The kind nurse held our hands as the doctor readied. "You're going to be fine."

We wondered if anything would be fine again. Annie quaked; the doctor took off his mask and said, "I'm not doing this. You're not ready." We listened to the vacuum. We didn't know what hit us. When the room went silent, we rose up in wonder; it had been so easy. The nausea was over at last. For Kita, the nausea from the chemo would go on.

We wondered if we would ever forgive ourselves. We didn't need anybody's forgiveness.

Every recliner in the recovery room was full. It was over; we looked up. Many smiled compassionately. Some felt theirs was the only good reason. Liz, who still had three AP exams, didn't know who she was anymore.

We wanted to hold hands. We wanted to get the hell away from these losers. We wanted to cocoon in our beds.

We longed for our mothers.

Some lovers promised: "We'll try again when I get a job." Cindy wouldn't have to cancel her Paris vacation. Carrie forgot to ask if she could hustle that night. We realized how much our husbands loved us. Jenna had to wait until child protective services came to pick her up. We were relieved that our grandchildren wouldn't see our swelling stomachs.

Joyce didn't have sex until she was married eight years later. Trish went back to work like nothing ever happened. We made a donation every anniversary. We were pregnant with memory for the rest of our lives.

We never thought about it again.

GHOST STORY

Thirii Myo Kyaw Myint

They wanted to meet a ghost. Sam said they had to add the adjective *benevolent* if they didn't want trouble. Sandy didn't believe in unbenevolent ghosts. Sandy believed in enlightenment, the Virgin Mary, guardian spirits, witch doctors, and celestial beings with glowing bodies. Sam was raised Catholic. They agreed that Catholicism was the best kind of Christianity because it embraced the grotesque. They liked to see Jesus suffering everywhere. They loved saints and relics and miracles. They said they wanted to meet a ghost, but if they had met Gabriel with his flaming sword they would have been equally satisfied. If they had met Tara or Ganesha or seen a rainbow body. They sought out enchanted places. Secluded woods. Hidden alleyways. Empty parking structures. They filled their apartment with mirrors.

They broke several of them. They walked cemeteries from midnight to dawn. Burned candles all night. They trespassed into old hospitals and dormitories. Got chased by street dogs. Dogs bark at ghosts, Sam said when they had managed their escape. Sandy was sure the dogs were wolves. They walked along the bay where the mob dumped bodies and children drowned yearly. They kept vigil beneath the suicide bridge. Railroad crossings where cars had been trapped. Once, they stuffed their pockets with raw meat and rotten eggs. The smell attracted vermin, but no ghosts. They slept in old churches and graveyards. They were robbed. The thieves took Sandy's wallet and Sam's gold ring. They were deep sleepers. Once, Sam felt goosebumps while passing under an archway and Sandy felt a breeze blow through a hall with no windows. That was all. They nearly despaired. They read tarot cards. Cast pennies. Will we ever meet a ghost? they asked. Sam drew the Ace of Cups, reversed. The seed of spiritual collapse, a missed opportunity for joy, contentment, fertility, or enlightenment, Sandy read. The I-Ching was no better. The things least apparent, Sandy read again, receptivity giving way to stillness and obstruction. How to unobstruct? they wondered. How to receive joy, contentment, etc.? Sam went on the internet to find an answer and Sandy went on long meditative walks. They came to the same conclusion. Most people only met the ghosts of their loved ones. Dead parents, friends, and pets. Who did we love? they asked themselves. All four of their parents were alive and in good health. Their eight grandparents were robust. All their siblings, all their friends. Spiritual collapse, Sandy said. Sam flipped through old yearbooks. It was no use. The veil will not lift for us, Sandy thought. There is no veil, Sam thought. What if we had a pet? they thought. Animals died young. But could we love our pet, Sandy asked, if we were only waiting for it to die? No, Sam agreed, we could not. Besides, they reasoned, they were not cruel. They could not wish for anyone's death, even the death of a future pet. They sat in silence in their apartment that night and did not sleep. The blue light of Sam's computer illuminated their living room. Who do we love? they asked themselves. When morning came, they had the same idea. They knew what they had to do. Sandy wrote their names on two pieces of paper and put them in a bowl. The two pieces looked identical. Sam reached into the bowl with eyes closed and withdrew one of the pieces. They held their breath as they unfolded the paper and read the name written there.

DOBSON UNIT

Alvin Park

It was about filling holes in the atmosphere that we couldn't even see. The men and women in white coats said it was the only way, that it could help the crops grow new and the tides swell again.

I told her this thinking she would be proud or happy or afraid.

She leaned against her front porch, her cigarette flashing the blank spot on her finger, a piece of gold we used to share, a piece of metal that ran through my hair, clinked against bed post.

She took a drag, blew out the smoke, said, When do you leave?

When we were younger, when the sky wasn't pockmarked with holes that let in the sun, we used to watch birds. She picked feathers from the grass, put them in her hair, tucked behind an ear. We went to museums and looked at skeletons. We said, Look how thin their bodies are. Look how hollow and fragile their bones.

When I learned to fly, she was the first one I took up. I pointed out the window and said, This is what they see. She held my hand and traced the mountains with her finger.

But after the tests, the needles poked just below her stomach, the test tubes we filled with ourselves, we forgot feathers and beaks, engines and wings. They said it had to do with the sky heating the trees, setting fire to the mountains, the sulfur sleeping in the dirt. It filled the air with poison, poison that said, The future is no place for children.

I said to her each night, I'm still here. I'll be right here.

But I wondered that I was, that either of us were, in that same bed.

The day that I was to fly up: I hadn't told her that I wouldn't be coming back. I hadn't told her that the only way was to plug the hole with more fire, fire that had to be guided until the very end. I hadn't told her that this may not work.

But we have to try something, they said.

Before I stepped into my plane, the men and women in white coats shook my hand. They said, You are a hero. You're saving this world. You will be remembered.

As I made my ascent and armed the canisters filled with

the chemicals that would heal our sky, I thought that I could make it all up to her now, that I could fill in the gaps and the holes, the people I should have been for her. I remembered that she was ticklish, that she laughed when I brushed feathers against her skin, when I said, We can both be weightless. We can both float away from here.

BEFORE

Amina Gautier

Watch them, they say—the parents, the aunts and uncles, the grands and guardians. They hand us off to the Olders—our cousins and siblings, play and real—as they pack purses, shine shoes, brush off hats and put on their Sunday best, although it is only Wednesday. Tonight they have Bible Study, ushers' meetings, choir practice, Masons and Eastern Stars, things they refuse to miss on our account.

They assign the Olders to keep an eye on us—the big brothers and sisters, the cousins, both play and real. The Olders draw lots and sacrifice two of their own, tribute to the gods that are we. A play cousin to watch us outside, a real cousin to watch us upstairs. At our age we wield power; we exude danger. We are unpredictable. There is no telling what we might do if left to our own devices. We might turn on the stovetop and watch the flames dance up to the ceiling. We might run the water too hot for our baths and scald ourselves to death. We might ignore the Mr. Yuk warnings and rummage through the kitchen cabinets looking for a poisonous drink. We might pick up the receiver, make long-distance calls, and run the bill sky high. We might take candy from a stranger.

They ply us with Mike and Ikes and Lemonheads, Jolly Ranchers and Boston Baked Beans, Now and Laters and Chick-o-Sticks. They plug in the Ataris, pull out the Teddy Ruxpin and Cabbage Patch dolls, the Voltrons and Transformers, the He-Man and She-Ra action figures, the Jems and GI Joes. They hand out jump ropes, marbles, skelly caps, clumps of colored chalk. Anything to distract us from what they are doing. They don't want us to follow when they creep down to the basement and pull out their records, don't want us to see when they sneak in friends.

The girlfriend of an older brother—someone who didn't know the music would carry up from the basement and cry out the porch windows on the first landing and flow out onto the sidewalks where we skipped rope, played skelly, and leaped hopscotch, who had no idea that the music would float up the stairs to the second floor where we huddled on the corner of the bed closest to the TV, joysticks in hand and pressed down on the red firing button to shoot the asteroids and alien centipedes that poured from the top of the screen—puts on the first record and forgets to close the basement door.

The music calls and we come. We bring our young bodies down to the basement door, to the mouth of the forbidden party.

This is no place for little kids, they warn, but we don't budge. Couldn't we cut them a break and just go back upstairs or go outside? Wasn't it enough that they couldn't escape us all day long inside the house, that they were forced to take us with them wherever they went, that we followed and shadowed and mirrored everything they did, that we copied them and the grownups thought it was all so cute? Couldn't they just have a little time alone with kids their own age without us tagging along, dogging their every step?

Ha ha.

"We'll tell." We say the magic words, no qualms about playing dirty.

"You guys are a real pain, you know," they say, in voices filled with all the angst of teenager-ness.

We know. We are the younger ones, born to be the brats. We expect to have everything our way. We have never been disappointed.

They guide us down into the darkened basement, which has been changed over into a teenage nightclub. We forget that we are unwanted as soon as we see the spread.

The washer's lid is covered in a towel fresh from the line, a makeshift tablecloth to hold the opened packages of Krackel bars, our Halloween candy gone missing. Six packs of root beer and cream soda, bowls of popcorn, pretzels, and potato chips top the dryer. Nothing impressive; nevertheless, we are impressed.

Someone changes the record. The new song tells us to dance, to shout, to shake our bodies down to the ground. We obey. We know a different version of the singer—the Jheri-curled, white-suited, open-shirted, posing-with-a-baby-tiger version. Not the one from before, the one who sang and performed with his brothers. This song is from before everything we know; before the singer's hair caught fire while filming a Pepsi commercial; before the white spangled glove and the military outfits: before he started keeping company with Brooke Shields, a chimpanzee, and that midget kid from *Webster*. This is a before we want to live in, to cling to, to clutch and to capture. This is before the inevitable end of the evening when the cars pull up and the lights turn on and we scramble up the stairs as others scramble out the basement door; before the inevitable end of our youth, when the ones watching us grow up grow apart from us; before they move away and leave us behind, returning only for holidays; before the house grows empty cold without them—the cousins and siblings, play and real, who watched us when we weren't looking; before the parents, aunts and uncles, grands and guardians string latchkeys onto lanyards and drape them around our necks, the way Leia did to Luke and Han in the ceremony at the end of *Star Wars* that somehow made destroying the Death Star akin to winning the Olympics. Before they say to us, "You're old enough now to stay at home on your own," and pretend we've won a prize, caparisoning us in adolescence. Before we bow our heads like Han and Luke, waiting to receive the latchkey, knowing we've won nothing.

CRAVING SUGAR

Monterica Sade Neil

I'm pushin all dese broccolis round my plate. My big sista Keshia won't let me lee da table, but she ain gon win. I keep thinkin da longa I push em around, she'll just end up tellin me to get on up from here. But she just keep starin at me. I roll my eyes ata.

"Jodi, who is you rollin' yo eyes at?"

"You roll yo eyes at Mama. Why I gotta eat this, anyway? Mama ain't even here."

Ha phone ring in da otha room. When she leave, I put a bunch of dem ole nasty broccolis in my paper towel and stuff it in my pocket. Then, I push my fork thu one of dem broccolis to fake like I been eatin.

I'm gon get Miracle when she git back here. Who tol ha ta leave me here like this? Who else gon eat my broccolis when she gon? She know she owe me. When she first got here afta ha moma got sick, my moma burned all dem white dolls out in da backyard and gave Miracle a doll dark as me. Miracle hated it and dat made me feel sad inside so I went in da garbage can and stole a Ken dat aint look too bad. She thanked me and hugged me even tho he was burnt up just a lil bit.

When she don't know I'm lookin, I watch ha talk ta ha dolls. She be whisperin. She talk to em real sweet like dey married but dey don't neva kiss each otha. I like it a lot, but then Keshia saw ha and said, "Girl, you so stupid. White men don't listen to Black women."

Miracle said, "Nuh-uh! That ain't true. My daddy listen to my mama. Besides, I ain't Black."

Keshia rolled ha eyes. "That's what you think."

Miracle looked at me and I just humpt my shoulders. I don't know any men. No men be round my house lisnin to me and my sista and my moma at all. Just us lisnin ta each otha. Sumtimes.

Keshia come back and say, "You gotta eat it 'cause Mama said you gotta eat it."

"Why I gotta do what Mama say if you don't? Why you carin anyway? You don't like Mama."

She look kinna sad. "That's what you think, huh?"

I tell ha, "It's true. She always yellin atchu bout yo lil

friend that you be wit all da time and you always rollin yo eyes." I roll my eyes like she be doin ta Mama and she laugh, real loud and free. It make me laugh and feel proud like I done a good job at sumpn.

She smile and say, "Eat one mo fa me an Imma take you ta da candy lady. We'll get us sumpn sweet."

On da way ta da candy lady house, I see Briana walkin from church with ha big sista Ashley. Dey goin ta dey Uncle Lenny house. She my friend. I don't say nothin ta ha tho. When we pass each otha, I turn around ta look at ha, and she lookin at me too. Yestaday, when we was at da park, she tol me bout tha lie she told ha moma when she seen da blood on ha good dress last Sunday afta she picked ha up from Mr. Lenny house. I wonda what kinna lie she gon tell today.

I see all da church people walkin round and ask Keshia, "How come erry time Mama start talkin to you bout God and yo friend that she don't like, you be yellin 'Praise da Lord, Ms. Mary. Praise da Lord!'?"

She laugh, but not loud and free. This time, it sound kinna empty like it's missin sumpn or maybe it's fulla sumpn else. She say, "I just wanna remind ha dat when she doin all dat hatin and all dat fussin and cussin, dat she praisin da Lord."

I ask ha, "But how can people hate and praise da Lord at

da same time?"

She stop walkin and look down at me real proud and say, "Maybe you should ask yo moma."

I'm kinna sad Miracle ain't wit us ta go ta da candy lady house. She tol me she ain't have no candy lady where she used ta stay at. I said, "Whatchu mean? All dem pretty houses out dere and y'all ain't even got no candy lady?"

She said, "We don't need one," and I ain't even say nothin ta dat cuz who don't need a candy lady?

At da candy lady house, befo Keshia ring da dobell, she say, "My friend that Mama don't like stay here and she look different. Don't say nothin stupid." I look down at my feet and Keshia lift my chin wit ha hand and say, "You ain't stupid. I know you wouldn't do nothin like that."

I nod my head. Keshia ring da dobell and ha friend a sight to see. I neva seen nobody like ha befo. She fine, but Ken doll fine. I wave at ha and keep walkin. I wish Miracle was here ta see dis. Blow pops, candy apples, hot chips, laffy taffys, lemonheads. Dey got evrythang in here.

I say, "Y'all got some mo yellow laffy taffys since da last time, but I ain't bring nothin but fifty cents, and I wanna candy apple too."

When Keshia friend speak, ha voice a lil deep, she say, "We don't want yo money in here. You can have whateva you want," and I wish Miracle was here so bad.

NEIL

I get six laffy taffys, three boxes of lemonheads, and two candy apples. Dey let me watch cartoons and eat my candies in peace while dey kiss and whispa on da couch. Errybody got a Ken, cept fo me.

When we leave, Keshia say, "Life ain't about hidin from nobody, but make sho Mama don't know nothin bout dat. Okay?"

"I would neva tell Mama I ate all dat candy."

SEE ME

Anna Cabe

The Dictator's Wife should have never trusted her husband when he told her the crimson-filled vial would quiet the shouts, the rifle fire, outside the palace walls. "Relax," he told her. She downed the contents, gasping at the coppery taste, before blacking out.

The Dictator's Wife woke up twenty years later, when intrepid staff members of the new regime found her cocooned behind a false wall in the basement. She was hungry, angry, when she heard the pickaxes. Soldiers of the republic had to drag her off one of the discoverers, still scrawny enough for his Adam's apple to bulge, to keep her from sucking him dry.

"I think you're a vampire, ma'am," said the new President's doctor, examining her in a heavily curtained room, momentarily forgetting that treating the wife of their former Dictator with any formality was verboten. She hissed out that no, that was impossible, but stopped, chastened, when dagger-sharp incisors slid out of her gums. She realized that was what her husband must have been doing down in the basement all those years, experimenting with ways to prolong their lives, their rule, before a bullet silenced his ambitions.

Over the next month, the Dictator's Wife was strapped to a chair, muzzled, listening to the new administration as they decided her fate. Twenty years after her husband's downfall, the government was still shaky on its feet; her sudden appearance was cause for alarm. Some suggested staking her, putting her out in the sun, putting garlic in her morning blood porridge. They pointed out her thousand and sixty designer shoes, her rapacious appetite for Dom Perignon and Kobe steaks, that she had not strangled her husband in their conjugal bed. Others said they should pardon her, let her live quietly on one of those rocky, isolated islands with caves seamed underneath. She had been a village girl, a beauty queen plucked from the sticks to be a feather in the Dictator's cap. What did she know of politics? A whole city's worth of people dead, tortured, or disappeared was enough evidence, others said. Then don't make a martyr out of her for loyalists to the old regime, they retorted.

A compromise was reached to prevent another civil

war. The President put her to work, to "pay for her crimes," he said.

The Dictator's Wife has a new routine. No longer does she serenade rapt popes, paupers, and kings with love songs to men and country. The President, once a movie star, has put his knack for spectacle to work. He built an indoor stadium on the palace grounds, which opens only on the last Friday of each month. Tickets, despite the high price, go fast; a lottery was instituted, so that all citizens could have a chance to watch. The country's coffers overflow from these shows; they're popular with foreign tourists.

Trumpets announce the arrival of the Dictator's Wife, in a car armored with bulletproof glass. Her guards let her out quickly, before speeding back to the entrance. Each time, she stumbles before righting herself, her teeth sharpening involuntarily. She can sense the blood of thousands, holding their breath.

A few minutes later, the entrance opens again, and serial killers, political traitors, corporate robber barons, journalist gadflies—the most unrepentant, the most bloodthirsty, the most loudmouthed—are nudged into the arena. The trumpets start again.

The Dictator's Wife had to be taught to play with her food. To not rip out their jugulars immediately. "It's a show," the President told her. "Make it worth their while." She learned quickly; hunger pangs are good teachers, sun and garlic even better. She long stopped feeling shame at the gore splashing the white gown they dressed her in. A diplomat's wife called her tacky once, when she thought the Dictator's Wife was out of earshot. Who's tacky now? she thinks, as she slurps from a student activist's throat, the blood dripping down her chin. She makes sure to bare her fangs at the stands once in a while, hiss, and soak in the collective shudders and gasps of the spectators. See me, she thinks. See me.

When the last ashen corpse hits the ground, she, black bouffant coming undone to her shoulders, recalls her old training singing for foreign soldiers, before her husband took her away from all that. Stand up straight and tall. Flutter her eyelashes. Lift her hands to her chest, where her heart once was. Never mind that her white dress is streaked scarlet, her face smeared with the same. Think of it as rouge. Lipstick. She has no jewelry anymore, but what does it matter? The audience is here all the same.

Their eyes are all on her, thousands of them, like stars in the sky. And she's the brightest one of them all.

She opens her mouth, making sure they can see the gleam of her teeth.

WOLF

Madhvi Ramani

I thought it would be nice, camping. Depends who you go with, I suppose. I went with Ben. There's a problem with Ben, but his darkness pulls me in. It glistens off him like a leather jacket, and he is crying, oh he is crying inside, and I am comforting him. That's what's really happening, beneath the surface, but if anyone were to watch us, they would see this: Ben and I putting up the tent. Ben criticizing everything I do.

"You're so stupid, Maggie," he says.

"Yes, Ben, sorry, Ben."

I take it, because it makes him feel better, and maybe I am.

So we get through it all, and it's not like those camping scenes on TV, with people sitting in the warm glow of a fire, roasting marshmallows and telling stories. We are out here, on a lonely lake, in fucking Brandenburg, where there are wolves.

We eat gherkins from a jar, and wieners from a jar, and then it starts raining.

"Fucking unbelievable," says Ben.

We sit inside, the mud around us getting slippery, turning into a swamp.

"Could this get anymore shit?" he says.

It was his idea. He's supposed to be on one of his runs to Poland—something that involves wads of cash, and a gun—but he wanted to take a break, stop in Brandenburg, enjoy the nature. He's a romantic at heart, really. I'm supposed to be painting, but there's nothing like one year of artistic self-discovery to discover that there's not much there. All I can produce are monotonous canvases of grey, white and black. I don't have the layers of experience, the depth of feeling, that unique vision. So I hang around with Ben. He sees the blandness, the lack of inspiration, the failure, and he hates it. He makes me feel it. He makes me feel *something*.

"You're so fat," says Ben.

"You're cramping up the tent," he says.

"God you smell," he says.

He enunciates perfectly. It's because he doesn't want anyone to know that he came from some dump in the north of England, where his first job was on the factory line making bottles of pop. So even though we're here, in a tent, in Brandenburg, everything is conducted in an upper-class accent. It feels worse that way. Like the queen is swearing at you, and if the queen swears at you, she must have a point. It must be legitimate. It must be that you really are shit.

The pegs are going to slip out, the tent is going to slide, we will sink into mire, slide into the grey lake, disturbed by a thousand pinpricks of rain. The rain is giving me the urge to pee. If it doesn't stop raining, if the rain doesn't stop pounding that lake, the lake is going to rise, overflow, flood.

Inside the tent, Ben is telling me that he will make me go out there and re-peg the tent if it all goes to shit, and can't I get my clothes off? Sex is all I'm good for anyway. He should have come alone. He's tired of my cunt face. He wishes he had a proper girlfriend but he is stuck with me, and nothing is very good or fun with me.

"I need to pee," I say, and move around him to unzip the tent. Rain patters my face. I walk around the side of the tent and pull down my jeans.

"Don't piss near the fucking tent," says Ben, sticking his head out of the opening.

"What about the wolves?"

"There are no wolves. I was only joking," says Ben.

But there are wolves. There are always wolves. In every German tale. In every story about a girl in the wilderness. I don't move. I don't care. I'm about to fucking pee.

Ben sees the look on my face and sighs.

"Here," he says, withdrawing back into the tent, "take the fucking gun."

I look at the dark object being waved from the tent opening, and pull my jeans up again.

I take it, and trudge a few meters away. Then, feeling bolder, further, into the woods. It gets darker. The canopy of leaves mutes the rain. Trees loom. Dark bark, dark mulch, dark smells. I move deeper into the woods, the need to pee disappeared. Maybe this is what I needed, some space, alone. I could live here. The wet earth my mother. Power in my hands. I prowl further. Wolf-woman.

It gets darker. A shape emerges between the trees. Slick dark coat of wolf. I freeze. My heart hammers. Its eyes spark orange, I raise the gun and *boom!*

Black crows squawk into the night. The leaves shudder, and then eerie quiet. Or it seems that way. The rain is still drumming, but like it's far, far away. I walk over to the wolf, but it's just a man. Ben, sprawled on the ground, blood oozing into the mulch, a lit cigarette smoldering nearby.

He's gasping—swearing probably, or telling me to call a fucking ambulance—but I just stand there, taking it all in. And I know. I know that I will watch his glinting eyes turn to black pebbles, his face become pale grey. I will wonder at every speckled stone and jagged rock that I pick off the ground and shove into his pockets, the tracks of his heels in the wet leaves, the slick of his blood in the mud, the shock of the lake as I wade in with his body. The billow of his clothes before the water plasters them down and they sink, down, down.

Those images will provide decades of paintings. Paintings rich with texture, shrouded in layers of secrecy, what critics will say conjure up the violent and vital force of nature with a cold and calculating eye. And I will remember, beneath the surface, that spark, the warm glow of that cigarette, fighting the darkness.

BETWEEN COLITIS FLARES, EXPECT THE FOLLOWING SYMPTOMS
Eshani Surya

1. Cheating, ingesting what should not be taken in
    a. Ex: bean salads; and gristly cabbage; and kiwi with all the tiny seeds; and corn; and peanut butter on crackers; and red wine bought to pair with the Alfredo pasta; and chocolate pudding in a fancy, metal ice cream dish
    b. Often, consequences remain unseen, biding their time, to be felt in the gut later

2. The body learns how to hold on to even the insubstantial again, the scale tilts
    a. A friend says, see this as evidence
    b. Of what
    c. Of recuperation

3. A lost friend, the one who took the patient to the hospital for a CT scan just a year ago, who sat next to the patient as

she ingested bottles of contrast dye to enhance the lines of her organs

    a. Why, because of my calls, isn't it? Too many of them, asking if it will return, my voice all rimmed with tears

    b. What words can you give to silence

4. A new language has been learned—the patient is at partial fluency, understanding the twinges of muscles and insides

    a. Also, of bile and the colors left on a tissue after wiping

    b. Beware, the patient can only interpret the signals, the demands for help

    c. She will never hold a conversation with her cells, but at least the body, constant companion, never quiets

5. Panic, as the patient tries to understand

    a. Fears that menses blood is the wrong blood, that it is coming from the rectum as opposed to the lush vaginal opening where the body is just performing its monthly self-cleaning

    b. An urge to reach into the toilet and handle the feces, to parse them out and verify that the tomato skin caught in the middle isn't a ripple of blood

6. Thoughts like:

    a. I've done enough, this next time, if it is cancer, if I need to die, I'll be satisfied

7. Thoughts like:

   a. Give me anything, God, except that pouch, that colon replacement. I know I am supposed to love all bodies, but I do not know how I will look at myself if I must collect my waste outside my body and deposit it with my two hands

8. Secret-keeping—before, there was no way to be close with another person without warning them about how the patient might get up four times during dinner to use the toilet (after the water, after the bread, after the meal, after the dessert)

   a. When it all comes back and the patient must tell her new friends and her new lovers, will she be a liar for her omissions

   b. Can she be loved, still, after that inevitable resurgence

   c. Or, the real question: was she loved in the first place or was that love only for those healthy, uncomplicated parts of her

THIS HOUSE IS OUR BURNED BODIES
Marlin M. Jenkins

Not ash. Fuck the mythic metaphor of rising, as if only the movement upward means new life. Remember: Grandma, I met you on that block with the blue porch. You, sitting. Always sitting. I don't remember the last time I saw you stand but it wasn't in that house. You say you will see me someday on *Jeopardy*. You say quit skateboarding, there's no money in that. But I know there's something in the wheels, in the bending of wood, in the stairs' creak announcing they're here, they have a voice, no matter how many times they're stepped on. This city is not for us. Is it? I want it to be, but I admit I left. Dad left. The car rolled to the stop sign and the carjackers, they knew. Can I blame them? There is something that needs taking. It might not be the car but we can aim bigger, anyway.

I'm walking downtown and hand a woman a takeout box. I know it's not enough. I want to hand her a window, a museum, a building. I want to be giving without a savior complex. I'm an asshole if I think I could save anyone, anything, but I do wish I could keep a stoplight in my pocket. Keep a boulevard in my backpack. Say, these things are ours. Say, this home is our home.

★

I dreamed of Warrendale again. I drove past the same corner again again again and it tilted. It bent. It didn't make a sound. Remember, neighbor: I saw you last on my lawn where we would jump and see how many times we could spin before landing. We waited for tornadoes. We played Power Rangers and I was Kimberly. Ninja Turtles and I was April. The reporter. In the dream I asked you why you left. I asked me why I left. I asked me why I can't write about home and see the city wet. It's burning. It's bright.

I didn't start running until I left. In the living room, I'm shifting on a plastic-covered chair and it squeaks. The sound doesn't rise—it expands. It wraps us. But not like a bubble, more like an aura. A transparent cloud. A fog through which we see clearer. We stand, together. We will be back but for now we leave the house. The steps creak on the way down.

FORWARD

We walk toward the stop sign. The sound comes with us.

★

When I left I left with a suitcase full of dog's teeth. Squirrel bones. A pocket full of tree leaves and strands from carpet. I wrote the house's voice on my body. Carved fissures where there were fissures. Tattooed the fading paint with blood.

I knew the houses. Grandma, this house is our body. Your body is a gunshot. My mouth, another gun. The city opens and it spills a mountain of powder.

★

Yesterday, I shoveled through the mounds of soot and called it Enoch, called it Elijah, ascension—not Lazarus, not stone rolled away, nor the storehouse filled with grain, a silent silo. My arms were blackened and black and backward past the library, past the museum until I discovered a trunk filled with tongues.

They had no questions. They told me a story about fire. They said, "Whatever you are, I am." They said, "We do not wait." They said, "You cannot save us, but it is because we need not saving, not grace—just the air, just the skin to lick, salivate on, to taste."

I was digested into the ruin's intestine, pressed my knuckles against the walls of duodenum, tried not to scratch anything—make no more damage to any more walls. I pressed my ear to brick and tasted the smoke. Wafted in the sound of chariots and caught a ride in the haze.

★

Grandma says, "Don't do dope. It's called dope for a reason."

I tell her I won't and at the moment it's true. She tells my sister she needs posture lessons. I tell her how much we know about slumping, how a roof can fold easy as cardboard, how last week I cracked an egg and glass came out, porous yolk with a membrane of steel.

She never says anything about grandpa drunk or working at the steel mill but I wonder how often those coincided. She says she needs to watch her stories. Each day. I leave and come back and each day it's her stories or *Jeopardy*. The category is *places in which you felt most alive,* or *places you know are still alive despite what you've been told*. I wager every dollar. I know this one, Grandma. I know.

ORIGIN STORY, TO BE WRITTEN ON THE WALLS OF MY CHILDHOOD HOME IN BLOOD

George Abraham

so it's the night of my seventeenth birthday: my two party guests—my crush & my white friend—& i went to a horror movie i've already seen bc the boy i found beautiful hadn't seen it yet, but i didn't mind really bc it was scorpio season & i was a Spooky Bxtch™ who liked Spooky Bxtch™ movies & the movie was good, the way white suburban afternoons were *good*... to say predictable & full of jump scares & after the movie we got taco bell, despite the horsemeat rumors, & upon arriving home my mother asked if we ate anything & we lied & she still brought out a plate of mah'shee, which my white friend found disturbing yet oddly charming, & that night, we cut the cake but did not eat it; the boy i found beautiful left early to see his girlfriend who, it is important to mention, was blonde & unremarkable & as soon as all two of my guests were gone, i retreated to my room as if i expected anything less of tonight than this typical empty—my parents falling asleep in different rooms; the boy i find beautiful falling asleep in different arms; the distance between my bed & his: the distance between my mother & ethanolic syntax; the dying tree shedding its lonely moss outside of my front window—yes, that night, dear friends, was the first night i considered committing suicide.

& i cannot say it was the first night i didn't love myself; i hadn't the language to diagnose this self-emptying, despite the psychology class that gave me words wrapped in sterile gauze & fluoxetine, despite my mother & the days she'd stumble out of the back door in search of a second bottle bc the first didn't put her to sleep in broad daylight & father, who doesn't believe in western medicine, says *therapy is for white people*, calls both of us ungrateful & blames me for the day mama crashed her minivan into a concrete pole after the sun caught her eye, or at least that's what she told the cop when really she passed out at the wrong bend in the road & when the cop asked if we, her children, felt safe with her driving us back, i wanted to say, i do not blame my mother for her dry drowning; the nights she'd remind me i was stuck in hell with her bc she couldn't leave, nor could she imagine the wings i'd engineer:

yes, i inherited my mother's hands: i know how to

disappear silent as the repentance after the prophesized bloodshed & i've come to understand that there are several magnitudes to silence: the silence after the first man i ever loved tells me he's dating a white woman; the silence after my father says pansexuality is *something the internet made up*; the silence after i scraped my knees on the church's uneven pavement & swore i saw my bones for the first time; the silence after another apology, my mother repenting to a god she loves even in drowning & aren't we all reaching towards some invisible sanctuary: something to call shelter when our language & prayers fail us; my parents once built me a sanctuary & it almost killed me; my mother found sanctuary in my father & it almost killed her; my grandparents found sanctuary in america after the home they called sanctuary was stolen & that too almost killed all of us—

    my mother tells the story like this: once, while visiting an amusement park when i was just an infant, a bird swooped down, stole my hot dog from its bun, & flew off; she says i broke down & sobbed into my empty bun, or perhaps it was my first lesson in forgiveness; i cannot remember it exactly, but i'd like to think that was the most honest history that was ever written abt any of us.

A GIRL TURNS TO STONE

Ruth Joffre

It happens more often than she would like. On the bus. After school. In the lake where the members of her basketball team like to swim after winning a big game. Once, she turned to stone mid-stroke and suddenly sank to the bottom of the lake, where whitefish darted between her arms like children running an obstacle course. Her teammates—well aware of her unusual condition—called the local authorities, who lifted her out of the water by crane; luckily, the girl had not been submerged long enough to suffer the damaging side-effects of erosion. Most often, she turns into granite—one of the strongest rocks—though she has been known on occasion to turn to quartz or marble, depending on the circumstances. After practice one day, she and a teammate grab dinner, just the two of them, and decide to share a strawberry milkshake. In the middle of dinner, the girl leans forward to take a sip from her straw, and her friend does the same, leaning over the table so their faces nearly touch. For the first time, the girl notices the light band of freckles on the bridge of her friend's nose. When their hands touch, the girl's skin turns a glorious shade of blue, a kind of brilliant azurite. The stone is cool to the touch, but it warms quickly under her friend's fingers. Later that night, in the privacy of her room, the girl strips naked and allows her friend to explore. She's charmed by all the different colors: the desert red of jasper, the ribbed greens of malachite, and the throaty orange of amber. With her tongue, she applies a thin coat of nacre to the inside of her friend's wrist, where it gleams, opalescent as a pearl. Overnight, this liquid nacre dries, like a pale, lustrous scab, which peels off on its own, leaving behind a patch of raw pink skin the shape of a button. It looks so sweet and new; the girl tries to kiss it, but her friend yanks her hand away as if burnt. The girl hangs her head and dresses in silence, finding—underneath the bed by one of her shoes—the dried patch of nacre. She puts it in her mouth, hoping she can reincorporate it into her body, but no matter how long she sucks, it refuses to break down.

PEÑA BLANCA, GUATEMALA
María Isabel Álvarez

I.

Vapor swells over our village like the breath of God's mouth. Our radishes grow on the slope of a hill tethered to the ground like the cord of an embryo. When the radishes crown, we feel the earth move and we know it is time to till land into labor.

Our neighbors beam at our yield and offer to trade their fresh corn—rows of golden teeth between husks of green. In the crosshatch fields below, children chase the cocoa trucks, pumping their legs over unpaved road, spinning clouds of dirt from under their feet as the truck beds swivel at the hook, arcing the air in cocoa seeds.

I watch from the hilltop as boys lunge at the air like leaping trout, hoping to catch a taste in the rain of seeds. I long to be one with the fish boys, to scuttle through the brush and brambles as if it were swaying algae. But my mother keeps me close, her chameleon eyes trailing the back of my head as if I were a speck in her periphery. I never leave home.

Then one day my father tells me before I find a wife I must first find my brain, and school, he says, is where it might be. With the help of our neighbors we pool together enough for a few pencils and a notepad, and on the first week of the first month of the year I start my first day of school. I am halfway through thirteen.

At school, I am asked to loop letters over paper, split numbers into cells, carry knowledge with me as if it were a fifth limb. At school, there are maps and charts and posters of children, every one of them more wide-eyed and chubby-cheeked than the ones sitting next to me.

There is a girl. Her skin is the color of tamarind. Her hair blackened ripe like wild chokecherries. She cups her hand over her mouth when she laughs and at times I wonder if I am the target.

We are classmates.

But we are not friends.

Her name is Xiomara.

II.

There is a boy. I feel him spy me with his panther eyes.

Each time I feel his gaze a strange heat swells inside me, but I push it back from where it comes. When he passes by he carries the scent of wet earth with him. My best friend pulls me close and we laugh at his wooden spoon arms, his teeth like mushroom stipe.

I don't tell her I dream of him at night.

In my swirling subconscious, he and I marry and grow radishes of our own along the hillside. But when we uproot them from the ground we discover the radishes are not red but supple pink, like the palm of my foot. Not heart-shaped but gangly-limbed as a ginger root. These strange radishes cry until I press them against my breast, until I wake with sweat pebbled across my forehead.

At home, I am asked to loop a sash round my waist, split chicken from feather, carry the weight of our village in a sack on my back. At home, I am food and warmth and comfort.

One day, my mother tells me before I find a husband I must first learn to weave. She extracts yarn from a tin box and teaches me to wet the threads with bark from the avocado tree. She shows me how to excrete juice from achiote seeds, how to powder color from coconut shells, weave the earth's entrails into our textiles. After the threads have soaked the dyes and dried to a fine grain, we sit on our knees at the base of the loom as if ready to worship.

We weave to forget our present.

We weave to remember our past.

We weave deep into the night until my hands cripple like the clawed foot of a quetzal.

III.

The rain in Peña Blanca falls heavy like the tears of a weaned child. Xiomara and I stand beneath the shade of a cedro tree while I wait for a moment to speak.

She talks of her home life—how weaving both frees and cages her like the rest of the village women. How it is both the creation of art and sacrifice of the body, in the same way, she says, the earth both nourishes and enslaves the men in our families.

The water dilutes the dyes of her skirt and now rivers of indigo and crimson splinter over her sandaled feet.

She looks away from me, embarrassed.

I want to drink the colors.

I want to feast on the fruit grown from the soil where she stands.

I search for a blemish on my skin, a scrape on my forearm, to show her that I, too, am imperfect. The graphite from my pencil has stained the crescent of my palm, so I stretch my hand before her as the rain washes away its pewter sheen. Xiomara stretches her hand out, too. Water slopes down her arm and skims off her elbow, her waters fusing with mine, into the spot where I know one day our radishes will bloom.

We stand together until the rain drains all life from her garments. Until the skies run dry.

MIRROR

Yalie Kamara

Khadi puts it on at night. The bleaching cream that smells of roses, raw chicken, lemon zest, calamine lotion, and steel wool. She squeezes the tube and applies its contents onto the sample area, a plot of skin. Khadi works the cream deep into the back of her palms with her index and middle fingers. She rubs the swirls of white cream until they spread softly across her evening skin like thinning Asperitas clouds. If the results make her feel as free as daybreak, she will continue with the treatment.

★

An unusually scorching climate holds this April afternoon captive. There is no air conditioning in the eighty-year-old bungalow on 43rd Street in North Oakland. A thin line of nude, sapphire sky peaks through the top of the living room window. The grass on the front lawn has been zapped so hard by the sun that it surrenders all of the green from each of its blades. It is now the color of Tina Turner's hair from the *What's Love Got to Do with It* album cover. Heat often changes color.

★

The skin around Khadi's fingers are both dark coffee and cream, as if one color battles for dominion over the other. She asks if my mother approves of the foolishness of choosing blond braiding hair. I say yes, lying through my sixteen-year-old teeth. Khadi adjusts my height by pumping her foot on the beauty chair pedal. She positions me in the direction of the sun, removes the kanekalon hair from the package and sighs. As if to admit that even with payment for this service, it still hurts. That honestly, there is no hairstyle fee that satisfies what she is being made to do my hair. She exhales like she is trying to blow out a fire in me. Or like is she trying to extinguish the blaze that crowns each of her cuticles. As if something in me reminds her of something in her. As if to say this is where her own hunger started. With a strand, a braid, then a whole head.

Today, her fingers will be buried in my rebirth. She begins to spindle the straw hair into gold.

★

She blocks the sun by placing the mirror in front of me. I watch her fingers speedily work down each braid. Hair between thumb and index and middle. Push. Up. Over. Twist. Under. Twist. And then the next. The speed makes her joints pop like tiny firecrackers in my ears. At each pause between braids, we blur into each other. Her obsidian hue pulls itself from her wrists. Splashes of beige paint onto her skin. I am staring into her reflection. Which is my own.

★

Together, we are golden tresses, jute skin, white pampas grass hands, burlap tinted everything, a million goodbyes from the trap of dark skin. Forever daylight. We search for a sun to ravage us through and through. From head to toe. A sizzle. A burn that chars and lifts us from our old lives. New colors scrape the lines on the map that threaten to lead us back to the homes we do not want.

★

I return to Khadi every three months to make me feel beautiful, which is to say, a bit farther from myself. Her skin burns from itself like a lit stick of incense.

★

Look at her hands and my hair—watch us braided into the other's dream. We are nothing when not staring into the same mirror. Nothing without the other's eyes. Nothing without the other's hunger. We are an endless wish to run away.

I WANT SO MUCH FROM THIS LIFE
Erica Frederick

There's this verse in the Bible, and I'm sure this isn't how it goes, sure I had it remembered wrong since I remembered it, but it says a part of the earth is red because thousands of years ago, Mars was a comet. And it looped around us, turned time around, and rained red parts of itself here on Earth.

Everything around here is red. All sienna clay and burgundy soil that ends, full stop, at the red-with-rust BIENVENUE A LA MONTAGNE sign that's an advertisement for a cellphone company. Daddy says this mountain's red because of war, says the land is cursed with the blood of all the people we killed here. I think it's red because this is right where those pieces of Mars landed when it hit the earth—right here, for us.

I squat in the dirt in front of our house and its cracked

foundation. My feet are flat on the ground and my bum is low, something I watched Mummy become unable to do, until one morning, without singing it in a warning like she'd always done, she just unbecame. Unknew me, and Daddy, and everyone else in this life.

I roll an old perfume tube back and forth between my thumb and first finger. It's scratched at every place it could be scratched and each scratch is embedded with red that I know by now can never ever come out. I wrap the neck of the tube tightly with twine, loop it around so it's long enough to fit over someone's head, and start wrapping up the other end.

While I'm wrapping, I look up at the at those high northern mountains that can't belong to us, can only really belong to those Haitians who aren't black, those people who can't see here from there. You can't hardly see anyone who's small when you're big. When you've got mansions, and children who've got everything.

I look down at my belly, it's stressing out the seams of this thin shirt. Every time Daddy plants an eye on it, he can't stop laughing. He'll call me a donkey and ask how I'm going to raise that thing when I don't even got a chest to feed it. I guess I don't know. I just want my baby to have everything. More than even this earth. I pick up the red dirt in pinches and fit it into the tiny opening of the tube.

I can see my girl running a bowlegged toddler run. She

doesn't know yet that she's got a planet around her neck, and nobody owns it. It's all hers.

NO FRILLS

Gene Kwak

Out in the No Frills Supermarket parking lot, Roscoe and I take curb. The parking lot is all cracked plots and crack pipes and sniff vials. Inside is all age-spotted old folks palming fruit, or Hessians in ripped-sleeve metal tees shopping for cheap hooch. Ground beef here goes gray fast and a big-laugh janitor in basketball shoes is always propping up a WET FLOOR sign even though he just dry mopped.

Roscoe heard he's going back for another tour. To deal, he wants to midtown bar crawl, but three bars and sixty minutes in, it's clear he wants to bolt over any easy going. Which, fine. We can down our fair share. We're Nebraska boys, born and bred. What's whiskey, but cask-sat grain water? Still, I've never seen Roscoe this wrecked. His walk is all wobble and falter. Stutter steps, but slow-mo, like he's a past-his-prime player with weak knees trying to show off heyday feints. He crashes over a parking bumper. Eats concrete. Scuffs his pants, his palms bleed. He sits down and starts hitting himself in the chest as hard as he can with his fist. Hard enough that I can picture the future bruises. Hard enough that the sound alone makes me flinch, like an older sibling dangling a wild-winged insect inches from your face. I can't even make eye contact.

I asked the lady at the VA if alcoholism was a symptom of PTSD. "It's a good possibility," she said. A brush by, a non-answer. Walking outside and not looking both ways before crossing the street and getting smoked by a bus, that's a possibility. I wanted: There's a good chance. Better than good. One hundred percent. Roscoe got pills: white horse tranqs to help him cope. He was also told explicitly not to drink. And sleep? Doc mimed a whole routine: yawn, stretch, beddy-bye, but Roscoe told me the truth was far from that easy. He had to cocoon himself in his basement with headphones, a sleep mask, and a brown-noise machine.

"Brown noise?" I asked. "Is that the magic tone that makes you shit your pants? Loosens stool? Releases the chocolate hostage?"

"Are you done?"

"Bye-bye butthole control? Okay, I'm done."

"No, it's just a different frequency. Meant to mimic

a dryer," said Roscoe.

His actual dryer rattled so bad it sounded like a noise-rock outfit that only played washers and loose change. This was his nightly ritual just to grope for a few hours of shut-eye.

It worked for a few weeks. Until he got another notice. The possibility of seeing Afghanistan sand again was good. Better than good. Definite. The only sure thing the Army could say.

I see tears in his eyes as he beats himself blue. Blood is streaked on his white shirt; it runs down his wrists. I don't know what to do. I want to scream, "Stop!" But he's so blown and in his own head, it's like talking to a sleepy child or a hungry animal; there are a few mewls of acknowledgment but they're acting on guts and blunted judgment. Grabbing him might be wise, but Roscoe outweighs me by sixty pounds. Last time I tried to physically restrain him, we were mostly joking, but I jumped on his back and he kept moving, easy as a kid hitching up his backpack to catch the bus. Someone snapped a pic, our mouths so wide with glee you can count our teeth: me with one arm in the air, the other holding tight around his neck. A cartoon of a cowboy on a bull.

Now, I don't know what to do.

So, I start hitting myself in my chest alongside Roscoe. We are in the parking lot of No Frills in the pre-dawn dark that's only broken by those halos of every-so-often sodium lights and it looks like we are staking our claim. Two men showing our domination over the space: proud chest-thumpers asserting ourselves over the used needles, the cracked slabs, the torn lotto tickets. The sound of flesh meeting flesh thuds across the lot. Crickets chirp. To passersby we would seem cavemen, Vikings, Maori warriors. Strong and cocksure. But if they look close enough, they can see how hard it is for us to clench our fists when we can't stop our hands from shaking.

SECRETS IN OUR CIGARETTES
Patriz Biliran

13 months and 19 days

We had our first smoke together at your place in Maginhawa, a nice little room in a big house owned by an old widow from a far-flung province in the South. She had already called our attention, puckering her lips as if to say Oi, pisting yawa, sinabi na ngang bawal yan dito eh. But you raised your ashtray and shook it a little as to say Eto talagang si Manang, hindi naman ho kami magkakalat, despite the ashes not being the problem. She shook her head but gave you a smile as if to say Ay sya, sya, sige na nga.

You told me I was pretentious—the way I smoked. I didn't inhale as I was supposed to. I didn't draw it into my lungs. I couldn't possibly taste its bitterness. I told you I only liked the menthol taste of the cigarette on my lips, and

I didn't want anyone to smell the nicotine on my clothes. I didn't want anyone to know. You nodded your head and made me coffee. It was dark and bitter.

17 months and 1 day

In your careful calligraphy, you wrote to me, *I wish you could learn how to love properly.*

I kept your note, shaped it like a cigarette, and three days later, burned it. I watched the flame engulf the paper quickly, indifferent to the words it contained. You left it on the table where we once had dinners together.

Your cabinets were now empty.

11 months and 29 days

My mother arrived earlier that day from the province to visit me. We fetched her from the airport in a car you borrowed from your sister's fiancé. I was supposed to introduce you. And yet—when she asked *who is this pretty lady?* I stood in shock and told her you're *just a friend* who's nice enough to accompany me. She asked about Chris—the guy I fucked when I was fifteen and the guy I usually fucked when I was drunk and confused. I told her we were still together.

I didn't look at you, and you didn't say a word.

3 months and 1 day

Your hair was the color of purple yam, and you were wearing an electric blue dress. I couldn't take my eyes off you. I said hello and offered you my lighter. You said thanks and smiled. Jokingly you asked me *what's a girl like you doing in a place like this?* I did not speak. I was dumbfounded, and all I could think of was your hair and the purple yam my mother used to bring home back in the province. We sat down at a table near the bartender and drank whiskey.

16 months and 15 days

When a song played in a local tongue you did not speak, I stood and took your hand. Around people I knew and people who knew me, we danced.

In the local tongue we both knew, I told you I love you.

THE EQUIVALENT OF _____

Ursula Villarreal-Moura

On the last full day of our honeymoon in Zagreb, Marcelo and I boarded a public bus to a casino located inside a mall. We'd been fighting so it hadn't occurred to us how vacant a casino would be at three in the afternoon. The sight of only a few truant teenagers loitering in front of the complex sobered us and confirmed our knack for bad decisions.

We had never been to Vegas, yet it was obvious this was a poor excuse for a casino. Aside from aisles of shiny red and gold slot machines, the interior was reminiscent of a pizza parlor arcade. Under a canopy of blinking lights waxen-looking staff stood dressed in pressed white-collared shirts and black slacks. Marcelo and I avoided each other's eyes while feeding the noisy machines. The number of awful or disappointing experiences we'd encountered on our honeymoon was approaching a fucking hundred.

After losing the equivalent of fifteen American dollars straightaway, we decided to comb the rest of the mall for cultural oddities. Since learning the modern-day tie originated in Croatia, we'd half-heartedly decided to find two or three stylish ones for Marcelo. The thing was Marcelo was indifferent to ties, so we idled about hoping to stumble upon specialty candies or newfangled household gadgets.

After strolling past a budget beauty shop and an artificial flower boutique we entered a battery repair shop with two display cases of silver jewelry. Marcelo and I both knew this mall, bleak and ill conceived, was a living portrait of us.

With a spark of optimism, he said, "I'll buy you anything you want here."

My watch still ticked, but I sensed he was trying, so I stifled a snort. This was possibly the first time either one of us had attempted tenderness in five days.

Standing in front of a revolving stand I inspected heart-shaped sterling silver charms and zigzag pins that had been popular in the United States circa 1987. Bad jewelry, I realized, is universal. Nothing remotely appealed to me.

The owner of the shop detected my apathy. He curled his finger for me to approach then retrieved a velvet-lined tray from under the register.

Rows of crude and chintzy earrings lined the tray like elongated fish. In the center was a pair of what appeared to be silver coins roped onto silver hooks. Kenzo, a brand I only recognized as a perfume manufacturer, was stamped on the back of each silver disc.

"Do you want them?" Marcelo asked. "Can she try them on?" he asked the owner.

The elderly man nodded with closed eyelids as if to indicate this was all scripted.

I tucked my hair behind my earlobes and slid the earrings in. The roped coins grazed my jawline and refracted in the mirror.

Marcelo appeared over my shoulder, the curve of his smile nearly lost in his overgrown beard. The thought *I hope we never divorce* formed like a fence in my mind, and although everything about the mall, Croatia and us felt doomed, I truthfully confessed, "I love them."

Under ordinary circumstances this might have marked a peace. But the next day, we squabbled on the flight out of Zagreb and barked sarcasms at each other while racing to catch our connection in Dublin. We left barbs and blame in every country, on half-eaten meals, balled up inside receipts, our graffiti on everything.

DADDY'S BOY

Dennis Norris II

I.

Open your mouth. Sing, boy. Rise up from your pew and praise Him. Take your hands off your hips. Don't dance, don't smile, just clap. Firm up those wrists and sing. Your mouth is His. Those lips? That voice?

Speaking of voice: make yours deep. No one likes a boy who sounds like a girl. Don't linger on the s's when you speak. The air whistles through the space between your teeth. It angers Him when you whistle like that, and when you place your hand against your chest and curl your fingers at the collarbone as if you are wearing a pearl necklace. You exist to do His bidding.

Boy, I see the way you prance around the house with that old baby's blanket hanging from your head, all the way down your back. I see the way you toss it with your neck, wishing your hair was long and blonde and pretty. I see how you swish around the house when you're feeling good, feeling proud, hips swaying side-to-side, prancing on your tip-toes. The other day, after you came home from school, I watched you pick pebbles from the garden beside the driveway along the edge of the house. You searched methodically, examining each one you chose, bringing them close. Selecting some, returning others. You took your time. When you had collected enough, you brought them inside and asked for the crazy glue and a pair of dress socks. I would've stopped it then, but it never occurred to me what you were up to until I heard you clomping around the basement.

You reveled in the rhythm of your homemade heels—that clicking across a hardwood floor that boys don't get to make.

Open your mouth. Rise up from your pew and praise Him. Sing for Jesus as His flock watches me drag you by the wrist to the front of the sanctuary. It's all right. I'm doing His work. Sing with us as I pull your pants down in front of everyone. Your cheeks are drums, my hands the beat. Cry as loud as you want. Your voice is His. We are making music, son, you and I, as I train you up in the way you should go!

I do this because I love you.

Because He tells me to.

Open your mouth. Sing, boy!

II.

At night—when we're on our knees in bed, his large hand between my legs—his ambitious thumb searches for a way in. His other arm wraps around my waist, pressing his chest to mine. My lips brush his neck. My teeth graze his ear. When he lays me down, his heart entering mine, the words climb from inside me, a whispered sacrament: cover me in you. I love him in a different way. He is better than those who came before him. You always said my life depended on Him. I think you were mistaken on the him in question.

It's important you know this: I let him do all kinds of things to me. He likes to hold me down flat on my stomach. He takes one of my wrists in each of his hands, spreads my arms wide, and presses them to the bed so my body forms a cross. With his tongue, he moves downward. He wakens my blood, wets every hair on my body so they stick to my skin. When he flips me over, he works his way back up to my ear, marking me with his teeth, his hands.

When he enters me he says, "Who's your daddy?"

He says you're the one who made me this way.

HOLOCENE: MICROFILM REEL 82

Kristine Ong Muslim

See the first *Homo sapiens* live alongside Neanderthals in areas later known as Syria, Lebanon, Turkey, and Israel. See how the exact reason for Neanderthal extinction is still not yet known, how sometime later *Homo sapiens* begin to have elaborate rituals for burying their dead. See Mary Leakey find footprints in Tanzania, proof that early hominids walked erect on two legs. See Heron of Alexandria invent the steam engine and write the first known book about robots. See Apollonius of Perga devise the mathematics of conical sections for use by Johannes Kepler eighteen centuries later. See Buzz Aldrin talk about the issue of inertia while on the moon, saying "I had to plan ahead several steps to bring myself to a stop or to turn without falling." See the docile birds, a gannet and a tern, that Charles Darwin discovered in

St. Paul's. See Gregor Mendel in the monastery garden as he tends to his cross-pollinated hybrid peas, the male flowering parts of which have been excised to prevent self-pollination; it won't be long until he observes a familiar pattern emerge. See Darwin scrutinize barnacles for two and a half hours every day for eight years—a routine that becomes so thoroughly ingrained in the minds of his children that they believe this is what men do, and so they ask kids in another household, "When does your father do his barnacles?" See part-time lab worker Alfred Sturtevant map out the distances between genes, laying out a scale for fruit flies' chromosome number 2: There's the gene for purple eyes, for short legs, for bent wings. See the stunned expression on the face of the first reviewer for Watson and Crick's historic one-page paper detailing the spiral-staircase structure of DNA. See the court martial of Cpl. John Mayfield and Cpl. Joseph Vlacovsky, the Marines who refuse to give DNA samples, arguing that doing so is an invasion of their privacy. See Alfred Nobel accidentally stabilize nitroglycerin with cellulose. See a close-up of human skin with chemical burns and huge blisters produced by exposure to mustard gas. See Albert Einstein talk about nuclear fission in his letter to President Roosevelt, kicking off the Manhattan Project. See Little Boy on its way to Hiroshima. See the five firemen who died within thirty-six hours of preventing more catastrophic effects of the meltdown at Chernobyl nuclear reactor Unit 4. See Heinrich Himmler bite into a cyanide pill just before his interrogation; his right hand is no longer shaking. See the court stenographer in one of the thirteen Nuremberg trials keep a straight face while typing a testimony describing human bodies being dragged from a gas chamber. See into the room-size vault where the stolen gold bars of the Marcoses are kept, lit by a lone 10-watt bulb. See the Tagbanuwa tribe drive away Mrs. Teo, who wants to build a SpongeBob theme park on their coral reef. See the Subanon tribe mourn the destruction of their sacred ground, Mount Canatuan, during the gold rush. See the human zoo in Coney Island, the cage labeled "savages." See Harriet Hemenway and Minna Hall, among the first refusing to wear plumed hats, file a petition in Boston to prevent the extinction of birds from unregulated hunting. See Jill Robinson in Sichuan province as she pleads for the lives of moon bears. See the Stetson family, one of them holding a selfie stick, pose with a lolling, drugged tiger seven months away from liver failure after repeated injections of sedatives. See the orcas of SeaWorld slowly driven to insanity by the stress of captivity. See the orcas of SeaWorld attack people when their counterparts in the wild have never done so. See the incinerator ash that used to be the bodies of people stricken by a deadly *Pithovirus* strain, which lay dormant for thousands of years until the thawing Siberian permafrost uncovered it. See into the ward where the index cases of superbug 01588:H90 wait out their eventual deaths. See the calm after the great flood of September 18, 2080. See the world no longer sullied by your presence.

HOW TO CATCH A SUN

Yun Wei

After her older cousin from the city told her that staring into an eclipse gives the ability to see into the future, Sun Huiyang looked. It was 1928 in eastern Sichuan, she was twelve, and the sun was a disk around a black moon. She looked until she went blind. Her eyes turned to milk and she couldn't see tomorrow or the day after.

At twenty-one, she married a man who liked to put his hands on her waist and tell her she had the ribcage of an opera singer. When he died, his family said it was her ghost eyes that gave him the blood cough. The way she looked at him. The way she never did. They buried her husband on an auspicious hill and threw her out pregnant after they finished the burning of paper money.

On the streets, she wove bamboo baskets, needles in her

fingertips, until the missionaries took her in because they saw a saintliness in her blindness and the jaundice in her baby boy. Her son was un-yellowed, got a Christian education then a city one then mathematics in college. When he came home from school, he talked of vectors and probabilities. When he left, he sent money home every month and tallied the amounts in a notebook stitched with cotton string.

Two wars and one revolution later, her son brought her to Maryland. It was 1995 and they went to the beach every weekend in the summer. Salt in her lashes, she explained to her four-year-old granddaughter, *Sun for descendant. Hui for kindness. Yang for poplar tree. I may have milk in my eyes but my back is always straight.*

The granddaughter laughed as if a great joke had been told. The girl ran to the ocean where the water began to froth. She came back with a yellow pail full of water and ground it into the sand between the old woman's feet.

Look, Grandma, the girl said, *I caught the sun.* A noon sun had dropped into the bucket, bobbing up and down like a beach ball. Sun Huiyang felt the mouth of the plastic bucket and dipped her hands in.

The water was colder than she expected. She could feel the loose swimming sand on her skin and traces of algae that hurried between her fingers. She saw the color red. A lit-within orb kind of red.

The red lanterns from her wedding day. The ones that hung from the sedan chair she sat in as they carried her to her husband's village. She remembered hearing the tap of paper against wood as the lanterns knocked in the wind. Now she could see them sway and flicker.

She saw the windshield flashes of white afternoon sun the first time she rode in a car in the passenger seat next to the missionary man, a sack of rice at her feet, drinking in the accelerated wind, bubbling from the swift sounds of leaves and gravel.

She saw the many faces of her son. The creases in his face when he cried. The smooth sleeping face after crying. Wide-eyed when he first went to school. Crumb-mouthed when he came back as if he were still hungry for something. The angry face when people asked him what was wrong with that poor woman like she was a deaf-mute hanging onto his arm. The noble face with pain pressed into the crevices when he told his mother he was going to leave because he had the chance.

She remembered how, thirty years after the eclipse, she had recognized her older cousin's voice at a town rally. Her cousin, a county official then, was giving a speech about meeting the end-of-year goal of smelting two thousand tons of steel, and his voice had a ring of such truth that the farmers rushed home to melt their pots and pans, and pulled the nails from their floors. Huiyang had stayed seated, and her cousin had come over full of pity and impatience for the strange blind woman alone on the long wooden bench. She could see now how her cousin's face had grown brown and oily with age, how the pockmarks had gathered as if grains of rice had been pressed in, then rinsed away. For a long time she had wanted to claw that face until it peeled off.

She thought of the last thing she saw: a white ring of sun she had wanted to slip into.

Two wars and one revolution later, she could finally fill in the colors. It was like painting a film long after it was shot in black and white. She pulled her hands out of the bucket and dripped them down the sides of the beach chair. There was a shaking inside her that she wanted to keep. She felt for her granddaughter's hand–that small, soft thing that must have been somewhere nearby.

Come here, little one, she said. *Let me tell you about the things I've seen.*

CIRCUMNAVIGATION

Maggie Su

The engineers of Planet Earth laid the tracks back to front and this caused a great deal of confusion—we'd think we were on the train to New York, but find ourselves lost in Istanbul. If we missed our stop, we could take the train past Sydney and slingshot around back to the park's entrance in twenty minutes, but it was still a point of concern for the managerial staff.

The day the trains shut off, we sat bored at the daily 11 a.m. huddle, next to a group of big bearded men who played tsars in Moscow.

"Can't you just change the signs?" we asked, but no one listened. They were waiting for the day's parts to be assigned.

It didn't matter—we were twenty-three-year-old girls and this job was nothing serious. We were busy printing out graduate-school applications that we never finished, taking shots of cinnamon-flavored whiskey at dive bars, making out with boys who sang in Weezer cover bands. We were just workers in Planet Earth, not guests.

Daisy was assigned the main performance, a tea ceremony in Tokyo. She was always your favorite—the only one who never forgot to put a spoon in the freezer before bed so that in the morning, she could press the metal against her eyelid to make a crease.

"Daisy Double-Eyelid," we teased and kissed her hard on the cheek.

In the locker room, we stripped out of our cut-off shorts and muscle tanks and stepped into red-and-yellow kimonos.

Today you were all men: VIPs in ties and cufflinks on a corporate retreat. It didn't matter to you if we were really Japanese or not. Most of us were born in America, second-generation, but for you, we pretended we barely spoke English. Our accents changed depending on the parts we were given: one day we staged Kabuki theater, the next we served pho in Vietnam.

Though we'd seen it a hundred times, when Daisy poured tea for you, we watched closely. We were proud of the straightness of her spine and her steady hands. How the tea's steam brushed her chin.

"You're so beautiful," you said when it was over. You

touched her white-powdered cheek with the back of your hand.

Daisy smiled without teeth and bowed like she was supposed to. When she turned back to the kitchen, she didn't know that the ends of her hair were clenched in your fist, and after a few steps, her head jerked back.

You kept her there for a moment and it looked like a dance to us, the long black strands stretched across the open space, taut as a kite string.

"Such fine hair," you said, before you finally let her go.

In the kitchen, we thought she'd cry pretty, but instead her thin eyebrows shook and her cheeks caved in on themselves. She smashed the teacups to the floor. She tore at her kimono until the seams gave way and she stood before us in nothing but black cotton underwear.

"Calm down," we said, but our hands shook, too.

Daisy stopped and stared at us. On the other side of the door, we could hear your deep-throated laughter, the sound of glasses clinking.

"Where the fuck are we?" she asked.

"Tokyo," we said. She shook her head and left us there with her mess.

By noon the trains had broken down, so Daisy must have walked half-naked through the streets of Planet Earth for a few hours before she reached the entrance, before she found herself spit back onto American streets. But she must've known then what we didn't: that really we'd been in the same place the whole time.

We wanted to quit too, to walk straight back to our studio apartments or, hell, maybe play tourist for a few hours—gape at the monkeys in Bangladesh or explore the mini–Congo River with the muscled men who played Pygmies. But instead we cleaned up the kitchen and smiled at you and after that, we were tired, so we waited for the train.

ESSAYS

PLANETS IN MINIATURE: ON KANDOR AND COMPRESSION IN FLASH FICTION

W. Todd Kaneko

In his Fortress of Solitude, Superman keeps a city in a bottle—Kandor, the capital city of Krypton, miniaturized and stolen by the villainous Brainiac before the planet was destroyed. *Action Comics* #242 (1958) features Brainiac arriving on Earth in his spaceship to shrink and steal Metropolis; after stopping him, Superman takes tiny Kandor to his arctic lair with the intention of one day restoring it to full size.

Kandor houses six million tiny Kryptonians, all living normally inside the bottle along with the surrounding countryside, forests, mountains, and some ancient Kryptonian ruins. Superman soon learns he can connect with his lost alien heritage because Kandor is his homeworld under glass.

A flash fiction could be called a little story, but not in the way that a dollhouse is a miniature of those mansions on the affluent side of town. While a flash fiction takes up less real estate on the page than a longer work, it can deliver an equal amount of story, just compressed. In great part, compression in flash fiction is not about shrinking, but about hyper-efficient narrative.

Example: See "Circumnavigation" by Maggie Su, immediately preceding this essay, a story about a group of young women working as generic Asian people at Planet Earth, an elaborate theme park that allows guests the illusion they are traveling the world. We meet the characters as they neglect uncompleted graduate school applications, take cinnamon whiskey shots at dive bars, and kiss boys in Weezer cover bands. We understand their youth, their lives in stasis, their capricious desires; we know them not because readers get to imagine what they can't see—instead, readers understand the lives they can't see because the story compresses these lives into these specific, vibrant details.

Similarly, Su reveals the story's size through its POV. She refers to the women in first-person plural *we*, while the Planet Earth guests are *you*. When Daisy performs a Japanese tea ceremony, she is assaulted by a specific man—*you*—and the women discover themselves reduced and objectified along with her. They are props not just in the theme park, but also in the real world. And as the story moves the *we* into direct opposition with *you*, the specific *you* shifts to a universal *you*, indicting not just the men in the story but the reader too. Their world blurs with ours and the story overflows out into our laps.

Calling a flash fiction like this "little" does the work a disservice because, while it's only 678 words, there's really nothing little about it. It's actually enormous.

Comics can convey a lot of information in a single panel because we pick up cues visually. *Action Comics* #400 (1971) features a story in which artist Curt Swan compresses lots of narrative detail into each panel. Kandorian students Arvor and Yllura argue about whether or not men are superior to women, and on display in the background is the "Annual Super-Scholarship Trophy" decorated with models of Superman and Supergirl holding a wreath. For Arvor, this argument is generally flirtatious—we know this because of how he smiles widely at Yllura and points at the awards on his sleeve. For Yllura, however, while the conversation is friendly, it isn't without seriousness—her smile is fierce as she proposes a friendly wager and points at the trophy, indicating her real goal.

Later in the story, when they are trapped in subterranean Kryptonian ruins, the illustration style moves from positive to negative space to signal a mood change. Swan's panels go from using bright, warm colors and detailed backgrounds to being completely blacked out with just wisps of white and blue, cooling everything down and plunging the characters—and the reader—into darkness.

Sensory information is nearly always filtered through language in text. In "Circumnavigation," Daisy is grabbed by the hair after the tea ceremony and Su uses metaphor to compress the assault to convey action as well as emotional experience. She writes: "You kept her there for a moment and it looked like a dance to us, the long black strands stretched across the open space, taut as a kite string." It's less a comparison and more a transformation as Daisy hangs powerless in the air, tethered to the fist of a man who seems willfully ignorant to her plight. The contradiction between the beauty of the kite's dance and Daisy's immediate peril has us on edge.

And the sentence is its own paragraph, suspended in its own temporal space, isolating the image from the next action—"such fine hair" the man says, then releases her. Time stops for Daisy and the reader, giving the metaphor a beat to come together before she is let go and the action continues. It's this highly efficient use of metaphor that creates and delivers the emotional value of this moment for both characters. Without metaphor, the moment risks being little.

FORWARD

Action Comics #400 (1971), art by Curt Swan

Superman eventually succeeds in restoring Kandor to its original size, but ruins it in doing so. In *Superman* 338 (1979), "Let My People Grow," the Man of Steel takes Kandor to a faraway, primitive planet and zaps the city with a reverse shrink ray. The people are restored to full size, but their buildings and civil structures collapse, leaving Kandor to rebuild society from scratch. Then Superman's Kandorian cousin Van-Zee punches him out and orders him to leave.

The cover of *Superman* 338 shows Supergirl trying to stop Superman from enlarging Kandor—"Your experimental ray may destroy the bottle city!" she cries. It's like she knows something about the value of Kandor's smaller state, something about how making it bigger will destroy Kandor's magic.

And perhaps this is true of flash fictions as well. They are so brief yet so immense, so effective and moving because they offer whole worlds for us to experience in so few words.

FOCUS ON FLASH FICTION
Alicita Rodríguez

Flash fiction abounds across so many countries and in so many guises: Greek parables, Argentinian fantasies, Icelandic sagas, Italian tales, Guatemalan fables, American short shorts. People call it a million things and undoubtedly the form is having a renaissance. I don't think its popularity is a mark of millennial life, an answer to a collective degeneration of our minds. Flash fiction doesn't exist for those who can't concentrate, because it is itself, at its core, a concentration. An act of distillation.

For a story to be flash, it needs to be brief. How brief is a long argument. At every length—500 words, 150 words, 50 words, 140 characters—there is something innovative that can be done with the form. I'm not a fan of short shorts that are merely condensed versions of a realistic story with a traditional narrative arc, although other readers enjoy that. I prefer flash that does something entirely different, whether it's imagistic, surrealistic, political, philosophical, or chronokinetic. I'd like to share some examples that illustrate the power of the genre.

Dino Buzzati tackles the form in "Falling Girl" by manipulating narrative time. Here there is an inverse relationship between the length of time something should take in reality (a girl falling from a skyscraper) and the amount of words the act takes on the page (about 1600). The suspension of time is further emphasized by the suspension of the fall, another interesting doubling: "Of course, the distance that separated her from the bottom, that is, from street level, was immense. It is true that she began falling just a little while ago, but the street always seemed very far away." Along the way, Buzzati also surprises us—the titled falling girl, Marta, spots another falling girl above her; she stops to chat with people on multiple floors (while falling); a young man tries to snatch her. And "Falling Girl" ends with another surprise that alters our understanding of Marta's flight/plight.

If "Falling Girl" is long for flash fiction, then Augusto Monterroso's "The Dinosaur" offers exceptional economy—at a mere seven words, it's considered the shortest short ever written. Part of its power, regrettably, is lost in translation. In the original Spanish, it's possible that we don't know who has awoken, the dinosaur or an unnamed person: "Cuando despertó, el dinosaurio todavía estaba allí." In English, the micro-story is less ambiguous: "When he awoke, the dinosaur was still there." Most readers will equate "he" with a witness-character instead of with the dinosaur. Still, there remains enough that is untold: readers are forced to imagine the rest of the story, thus making "The Dinosaur" an act of co-creation.

Luisa Valenzuela uses the genre to haunt us. In "I'm Your Horse in the Night," a woman is in love with a revolutionary. Where? In an unnamed Latin-American country. It could be anywhere. Her lover, whom she calls Beto, shows up unexpectedly after "all those months when I had no idea where he could have been." He gives her gifts, they make love, he disappears. Later she is imprisoned and tortured (which all happens in parentheses). When the police interrogate her, she gives up nothing, "deeply convinced that I'd dreamed it all... And dreams are none of the cops' business."

In the same part of the world, Carolyn Forché gives us "The Colonel," an autocrat who seems harmless enough until he produces a bag full of human ears: "I am tired of fooling around he said." This piece rests on poetic imagery. Forche's synecdochic ears come alive, become volitional, listening to the dictator in fear: "Some of the ears on the floor caught this scrap of his voice. Some of the ears on the floor were pressed to the ground."

Flash fiction is also a form distinctly capable of self-referentiality. Julio Cortázar's metafictional masterpiece "A Continuity of Parks" presents a man reading a thriller, getting lost in the story: "He tasted the almost perverse pleasure of disengaging himself line by line from all that surrounded him." Unfortunately, he himself is a character in the book he's reading—a character who is about to be murdered. How can we suspend our disbelief when we are faced with a man who can't suspend his?

If we want to get philosophical, let's consider Jorge Luis Borges, a master of fiction who consciously chose the short story and intentionally rejected the novel his entire life. In "Borges and I," he is a man with a doppelgänger, trying to survive while the other Borges, the writer, takes over: "I live, let myself go on living, so that Borges may contrive his literature, and this literature justifies me."

Flash fiction is paradoxical because the constraint of compression ultimately frees writers. Fewer words force a writer to stretch beyond—to expose a story by other means. When there is no time for plot, stories can subvert it, as with "Falling Girl," which suspends time, and "The Dinosaur," which encapsulates it. Without the space for character development, characters can become universal. Such is the case with Valenzuela's political dissident and Forché's ruthless tyrant. Cortázar and Borges use flash to examine the nature of fiction. In "A Continuity of Parks," the wall between reader and story gradually crumbles; in "Borges and I," the author's very identity is called into question. Flash gives writers the freedom to explore, and often upset, the conventions of fiction—expanding our notions of narrative and enhancing its potential.

ON THE SHORT FORM
Marcos Gonsalez

There's form, and then there's content.

So the story goes.

In my Latinx Literature course, I teach Sandra Cisneros's magnus opus, *The House on Mango Street*, and I pair it with Jean Toomer's modernist classic, *Cane*, to show a precedent to Cisneros's work, to show how others have taken to the short form. Toomer identified the prose pieces in *Cane* as sketches, Cisneros as vignettes, and critics identify both works as composite novels or short story sequences because of how the pieces are interlinked. The question of form continued to resound in the classroom, and the question of content, and the two remained two different questions. That is, until a student questioned how the shortness of the pieces represented the kind of psychic experiences Cisneros's protagonist Esperanza was going through, and the kind of elliptical, fragmented subjectivities Toomer's short prose was depicting. Her inquiry opened up room for thinking about form and content.

Students in literature classes are often trained to read content and form separately. Scratch that: literature students or not, that's how most of the world is trained to read. Form is not content, and content is not form. However, for Cisneros and Toomer, via flash fiction, form is content and content is form. And there is a risky, and dangerous, ambiguity to their merger of the two, to the smallness form and content create. Toomer's modernist sketches of Black life in America are elliptical, and fragmentary narratives, if possessing narrative at all. "Carma, in overalls, and strong as any man, stands behind the old brown mule, driving the wagon home," begins the sketch titled, "Carma," where, like many of the sequences in *Cane,* Toomer writes highly impressionistic externalizations of the characters in his sequences. There is a kind of faraway view of them, of Carma, of Rhobert, of Karintha, these people whose characterization becomes the plot, the narrative, the pacing. The profiles of characters abound in a kind of aimlessness, tracking the everyday: working in cane fields, women dodging the advances of men, the white lynch mob ready to strike. There is a sense of continuity, ongoingness in each piece, and calling them a short story, a story that has a beginning, middle, and end, would rob the kind of work these short pieces are doing. Sketches, then, are a fitting name for what Toomer is doing: glancing, skirting, and immediate impressions of a people, a community, the being that is being Black in the United States.

Cisneros, in distinction from Toomer, relays the inner workings of Esperanza as she tells us about those who live in the Mexican and Puerto Rican neighborhood in Chicago. Many of the pieces feel monologue-esque, Esperanza narrating the events and people around her and, like in Toomer, many of the vignettes are character profiles. In "Marin," for instance, Esperanza tells us about Marin, a Puerto Rican woman living in the neighborhood, who "under the streetlight, dancing by herself, is singing the same song somewhere. I know. Is waiting for a car to stop, a star to fall, someone to change her life." Bits of neighborhood gossip, a recounting of a past event, details of a life fill up the half-pages and one-pages that constitute many of the vignettes in *House on Mango Street*. Cisneros, in so few words, in such short prose pieces, turns a neighborhood into a universe, immigrant and Latinx lives the stars and planets.

Together, Toomer and Cisneros undertake two vastly different approaches to form and content. For Cisneros, it is a close-up of her characters, their inner workings, through the eyes of Esperanza. For Toomer, it is at a remove from his characters and setting. Thinking about these two works together allows us to understand how capacious the short form can be, how capacious it should be. Characterization can be a plot, and a monologue can be narrative. Both can tell a story (a character profile, an impression, a memory) in half a page, a page, or several pages. At the heart of both is the guiding principle that the short form is open-ended, adventurous, willing to hold the unruliest of subjects, the most delicate of lives. In Toomer's "Rhobert," a man with "an Adam's-apple which strains sometimes as if he were painfully gulping great globules of air…air floating shredded life pulp." This Rhobert, who seems burdened, life dragging him down, we know less of who he is, of his desires and life, than we did before we opened the page. This Rhobert is brought onto the page to be made more allusive, less known, a mystery of prose open to interpretation much like Cisneros's Sally: "the girl with the eyes like Egypt and nylons the color of smoke." Who is she? This girl named Sally who Cisneros gives two vignettes to, a girl who recounts to the narrator that her father never hits her that hard, a girl who recounts bits and pieces of abuse. What is the whole story for Sally? What defines her in such few words? This openness is profound for the kinds of experiences *Cane* and *House on Mango Street* represent, for the Black and Brown lives centered as their form and content.

The brevity of the short pieces in these two works caused a crisis for my students and me. How to categorize these two works? Are they sketches, vignettes, short stories? How to do we discuss the form and the content of these pieces when they elude the normative structures of storytelling? When there is no sequential narrative, no beginning, middle, or end, no decipherable causality? These questions merely expanded by the end of class. They carried into the next, into the rest of the semester, into our understandings of how flash fiction, how short stories, how novels, how poetry, how theatre, how the literary operate. Or how it can operate. The short form—the sketch, the vignette, the short story, whatever other words one may call their short work—is, to be grand about it, utopic. The short form is ideal for how it can show us different ways of experiencing time and narrative, more expansive and nuanced takes for representing people of color on the page because, through the short form, we can have our inner monologues if we desire, or we can have our at-a-distance glances if we choose. We are entitled to be elusive, to be fleeting, to be brief and immediate, to go in and out of view in an instant, to disappear from the page as fast as we came onto it.

THE SENTENCE TURNS BACK: JAMAICA KINCAID'S "GIRL"

Allison Noelle Conner

In *The Iliac Crest*, Cristina Rivera Garza writes "Something happens to the world when you turn back." The last two words conjure Cher: "If I could turn back time." Orpheus turns back and loses his beloved, Eurydice, to the underworld. The phrase "turn back" combusts with meaning: to return, a spatial direction; to abandon, a symbolic gesture. Does a sentence return us to a place and time? Or does it only strive towards a departure from the present and the self?

I've been thinking about the sentence and memory and retreating and inheritance because I've been poring over "Girl" by Jamaica Kincaid.

The editors at *The New Yorker*, where "Girl" was first published in 1978, offers this description: "a young woman's experiences growing up in the West Indies." Based only on the title and brief summary, you'd assume predictable grooves will follow, and on the surface, they do. The story involves a mother and daughter, but unfolds within a single sentence. Kincaid opens with commands linked by semicolons that resemble a needle's hook, crocheting together a patchwork of childhood sensations and disruptions. The sentence is all dialogue: a mother passing on to her daughter the rules, expectations, chores, warnings of Antiguan femininity: "this is how you sweep a corner…don't eat fruit on the streets—flies will follow you." Wash, cook, soak, grow, mend. The daughter speaks twice, to refute an accusation and to ask a question. When the daughter speaks, her voice is italicized, in arch defiance to her mother's instructions.

Kincaid's sentence is not merely a grammatical tool, a way of getting from point A to point B; it is an energetic bog of memory. A sly trick of the tongue. It follows a pattern of sorts (Wash, cook, make, sew. Don't. This is how.), but Kincaid sculpts the prose into a looping carnival: rowdy, full of reversals, attended by an undercurrent of peril. The mother imparts a lineage, a way of moving through the world so as to ensure spotlessness and protection. Being a "good girl" is very important to her. Kincaid infuses the domestic chores with a musicality, lulling you into sedation with its quotidian hum: "when buying cotton to make yourself a nice blouse, be sure that it doesn't have gum in it, because that way it won't hold up well after a wash." It sounds like a cheeky how-to, recalling the conduct manuals popular during eighteenth-century Britain, texts marketed to young women as an antidote to the supposedly corrosive effects of novel-reading. These conduct manuals guided their readers towards a strict "proper femininity" via cloying advice on beauty, clothing, social manners, dancing, romantic behavior, and more. "Girl" echoes this genre, reflecting the complicated dance between Antigua and its former colonizer, Britain. Here is another reading of what's passed down, whether we want it or not.

That unwanted inheritance surfaces as unwanted advice. "[O]n Sundays try to walk like a lady and not like the slut you are so bent on becoming." This is the first slap, out of nowhere and unsettling, a reminder that we are not on familiar grounds. The sentence is alive and accusatory. The mother mentions washing often, reminding her daughter to remain pure in mind, body, and soul. This narrative of femininity is restrictive, often seeming like punishment for a profane waywardness. To be sentenced. Suspended between madonna and whore. But Kincaid isn't keen on slick dichotomies, so there are moments of push back, of saltiness, of peeks into ancestral reservoirs and improvised agency. There are references to abortions, bullying men, and "how to spit up in the air if you feel like it." Who will the daughter become? The sentence feels like a long sigh, a release of psychic and emotional buildup. The mother needs to say it all, if only to give a little of what she's been holding. It's like the swirling maternal voices in Gayl Jones's *Corredigora*, urging the eclipsing importance of future generations to daughter Ursa, for she must bear witness to their horrific abuse. The daughter in "Girl" must bear witness to a genealogy of sublimation, to duties and rebellions and swampy zones between.

The compactness of flash means Kincaid must be acrobatic in her approach to character and tension. The sentence becomes a vessel: one false move, and the whole delicate balance splits into a terrifying plunge. Kincaid doesn't waste time explaining things to us. The texture of what's said, the specificity of what's done achieves a lived-in-ness of setting and community, capturing the vertiginous expressions of and reactions to gender dynamics, class, lineage, self-actualization. Kincaid places us amongst the working class, specifically the women tending to their invisible but vital labor, and the social rules over-governing their existence.

But the sentence holds the capacity for reconciliation, and involves a process of stretching time and memory to its breaking point, making from its pieces a collage electric with the kindling of past, present, future. Can a sentence turn back, and if so, what happens to the word? The word becomes an echo, transmitting layers of subtextual feedback. "My mother wrote my life and told it to me," Kincaid said to *The New York Times*. I keep overlaying this quote upon "Girl." The mother's attempt to speak her daughter's life. The daughter's attempt to write her mother's life. Kincaid's sentence could be instructions in femininity, a woman's recollection of her mother's lessons, a performative haze of obedience and skepticism. The meaning isn't stable, prone to perpetual shedding of skin, an apt expression of the restless tides of girlhood.

EDITORS' ROUNDTABLE

Leland Cheuk authored the story collection *Letters from Dinosaurs* (2016) and the novel *The Misadventures of Sulliver Pong* (2015). His newest novel, *No Good Very Bad Asian*, is forthcoming from C&R Press in 2019. He runs the indie press 7.13 Books and is fiction editor at *Newfound Journal*.

Tyrese L. Coleman is a fiction writer, essayist, and reviews editor for *SmokeLong Quarterly*. Her flash has appeared in *Vol. 1 Brooklyn*, *Tahoma Literary Review*, *PANK*, *Brevity*, and elsewhere. A Kimbilio Fiction Fellow, her collection *How To Sit* debuted in 2018 with Mason Jar Press. Reach her at tyresecoleman.com or on Twitter @tylachelleco.

Bix Gabriel is a writer, teacher at Butler University, fiction editor at *The Offing*, co-founder of TakeTwo Services, occasional Tweeter, and seeker of the perfect jalebi. Her essays have been published in *Electric Literature*, *Guernica*, and others, and her fiction in *Jellyfish Review*, *SmokeLong Quarterly*, and more.

Tara Campbell is a Kimbilio Fellow, fiction editor at Barrelhouse, and MFA candidate at American University. She is the author of a novel, *TreeVolution*, and a collection of poetry and fiction, *Circe's Bicycle*. Her third book, *Midnight at the Organporium*, will be released by Aqueduct Press in 2019.

Why and/or how did you get started editing?

Leland Cheuk: I would say I started by editing my own work as if it was not my own. I think you have to be a very strong editor of your own work if your work is going to be published these days because publishers are doing less and less editing. But the authors publishing on my indie press 7.13 Books can probably attest that I go at their manuscripts hard.

Tyrese L. Coleman: I wanted to get better insight into what journals want and the type of submissions that people send into literary magazines in order to improve my own writing. I started off as the fiction editor for *District Lit* after seeing a call that they were looking for an editor. It became clear, just on a basic level, that many people submit stories well before the stories are ready to be read by others. I also learned how to tell when a story was going to be worth reading all the way through and when a story might not be worth that same level of attention. I started working with *SmokeLong* because I love everything about flash and wanted to work for a team that focused on a genre that I not only write, but one that is established within the literary community it serves. I knew Tara Laskowski. She knew I wrote flash and that I edited for another journal. She invited me to apply for an editor position. I was lucky enough to have been selected to join the team and it's been an amazing experience so far.

Bix Gabriel: I wasn't sure if I wanted to work at a literary magazine, but I did want to get "behind the scenes," and understand how decisions about submissions are made, and what contemporary writers are doing with their writing. My friend (and now, co-editor at *The Offing*) Megan Giddings sent me a call for readers at a newly-established online magazine that was actively looking for work "by and about those often marginalized in literary spaces," and that cinched it. I applied and started as a reader at *The Offing* in 2015, and gradually became an editor. I love what I do but don't know if I would have lasted at a lit magazine (it is hard, time-consuming, and unpaid work) if I wasn't getting to read, edit, and publish some of the most exciting, new work by writers of color, LGBTQ, and others often underrepresented in the lit world. Plus, I'm very lucky to be part of a wonderful crew at *The Offing*.

Tara Campbell: My path to editing began with my involvement in the Washington, DC, literary community. I'd been writing seriously for a couple of years when I attended *Barrelhouse*'s Conversations and Connections conference. The following year, I volunteered to round out a panel on speculative fiction in which the moderator was looking to hear from writers of color. Later I was invited to participate in an online holiday issue, and gradually got to know the other editors. I applied to moderate my own conference panel, and over time became more integrated into the *Barrelhouse* community. When they asked me to come on as an associate fiction editor, it was because 1) they already knew me and my voice, and 2) they were serious about diversifying their editorial staff. After about a year of reading submissions and learning their process, they asked me to be one of the fiction editors—which, of course, I was happy to do!

What advice would you give specifically to writers of color who are just getting started?

LC: Be your truest self and write what you want, the way you want. Don't try to write what you think publishers want writers of color to write.

TLC: If you can join an editorial staff, do it. Reading submissions completely changes the way you read your own work and the way you write. It also helps to have an inside view into how the submissions process works. Everything is subjective, so being on the inside of such a subjective process helps you learn how to cope with rejection better. I think for many writers of color, being rejected is much more complicated. We could be rejected because editors do not understand the point of view of what we create or because we are being true to a cultural reality that white journal editors do not get. Seeing how the process works from the inside can help you see that, most of the time, rejections are not a reflection on talent but rather some other administrative issue. Additionally, having more writers of color as editors will inevitably lead to more writers of color being published. I have to say that I believe I've had an impact on that for the journals I've worked for and I hope to continue to effect change in this way.

BG: Some of this is advice I don't exactly follow, but aspire to! Read as widely as you can. Read outside the canons. Read outside genres/styles you like. Read new stuff, old stuff, stuff you gave up on. Read poetry, no matter what you write. Find a mentor or form a group with writers whom you trust. Writing as a writer of color is full of self-doubt, and lack of (external) validation. Find people who can cheer you, and help you, and genuinely care about your writing and you as a person. Try and join a lit magazine. It helps to learn how many magazines work. Or try an internship at a small or large press (though large presses are quite siloed, and you may never get any insight into the editorial process). Get off Facebook! Well...if you're finding yourself seduced or intimidated by the success and connections of other writers. Otherwise, social media can be a good way to know what's happening in the lit world.

TC: Being part of different literary communities has been very helpful. I've been in science fiction-focused groups and general fiction groups, as well as groups for writers of color. POC have always had to toggle between identities, and it's the same in writing too. It can be helpful to see how different audiences understand your work—not to say you have to change your message, but knowing *how* different readers arrive at their conclusions is a powerful tool. I would also encourage diversity in the literary circles you cultivate. I've enjoyed volunteering with various creative writing conferences and non-profits in the area, serving kids and adults. You learn about a range of opportunities in these different circles, which gives you more latitude to pursue the ones that make the most sense for you, rather than feeling you have to squeeze yourself into someone else's box.

What makes (or made) you fight for a story from the submissions queue to be published in the magazine that you worked at?

LC: I'm lucky in that I'm the ultimate decision maker at my press and with the fiction section at *Newfound*. I fight for stories that are different and urgent and need to be told because they haven't been told before. Right now, a lot of those stories are by people of color.

TLC: I've fought for stories that show a different world or culture that is not typical of what we normally receive in our submission queue. I am a sucker for language and voice. If I am struck by the voice or the language in the work, I will fight for the piece. More recently, however, I am finding that I am fighting against stories that other editors on our team are rooting for. Not because I want to be argumentative, but because I am looking at these stories from a different lens than they might be. For example, I have been highly critical of violent stories that seek to create sympathy for someone who is inflicting harm on another without examining the impact of that person's action on others. Just as important as it is to fight for the stories we love, we also have to be hyper-critical of what we support and the themes that we promote.

BG: I'm lucky that I rarely have to fight for a piece to be published, because editorially, though our team of readers and editors have different tastes and styles, we're usually on the same page about what we want to see in the magazine. *And*, since we're a team of all-women, most of us of color, the feedback or resistance to pieces tends to be for reasons one or another of us might not have thought about, and is usually spot-on. Our challenge is that we'd love to publish more fiction, but we simply don't have the funds.

TC: The stories that capture my attention are the ones that manage to balance a coherent narrative with a dose of the surreal. I want to feel grounded enough in some kind of structure that I can enjoy the sense of being thrown off-kilter when the rules shift in a bizarre way. The tastes at *Barrelhouse* are eclectic enough that we wind up discussing a wide range of work. There are so many good stories out there, it's often a process of elimination, gradually weeding out the ones we're less wedded to. But yes, sometimes we have a couple of people who are really into a story, and a couple of people who aren't as excited by it. So far, we've found a way to agree, so that even if each individual editor wasn't equally in love with every story, we're all happy with how the publication as a whole comes together.

What advice would you give to editors or institutions who are working toward making their magazines or events more inclusive?

LC: Consider diversity more diversely. A lot of the stories being celebrated these days are at their core very similar. What about POCs who are writing outside of the naturalistic, social realistic idiom?

TLC: Solicit diverse writers, readers, and editors. Don't take a piece of work for face value. Even if it sounds as if it was written by an #ownvoices writer, do some basic research into who the writer is. It is important that if you present work that is culturally specific that that piece is authentic and not a parody of someone else's culture.

BG: Investigate why you want to make your magazine "more inclusive;" if it's for tokenism, or not to get flak from readers, that will make it hard to find, read, and genuinely appreciate writers whose identities and writing differ from yours. Question your belief in the validity of blind reading submissions. When planning an issue or an event or even your editorial calendar, and masthead, make specific commitments to what diversifying your magazine or institution looks like, and honestly, try and go for equity! Be transparent about your goals. Talk to, listen to, connect with, read, and get to know writers and editors who are outside of your in-group. This takes time and work and honesty. Be prepared to fuck up. It's part of relearning/unlearning.

TC: I'd say it's better when it's a conscious effort over time, rather than a quick fix with a figurehead. It would be a bad idea to rush in a POC editor and call it done, because if your sensibilities don't mesh, it's not going to be a beneficial relationship for either side. Consciously publishing POC and other marginalized groups can be the beginning of a process of broadening readership and community, which can lead to a more solid and sincere sense of inclusivity. You can be intentional, but you can't put it on fast-forward, or it won't ring true.

What is the one short story—any!—that you wish you had been able to publish? Why?

LC: I loved the recent flash fiction in *The New Yorker*, "Break" by Rabih Alameddine. It covers a lot of emotional ground in a few words, and is about a pair of siblings estranged by one's gender transition. It's a story that's not political but filial, and both siblings are reaching for each other. It's a good example of considering diversity more diversely.

BG: Ah! A few months ago, I read a story in *AGNI* by Maisy Card, and fell in love with her writing. I got in touch with her and asked her to send us a story to consider. She did, and I loved this story. It shifted point of view, and had a strange, compelling storyline. But it took a little while before we could accept the story for publication. At that point, I learned from Maisy that we could no longer publish that story. Because she had sold a book, and her agent didn't want any other stories published before the book came out. So, yes, I was sad for us, but happy for her!

TC: That's tough. It's hard to choose just one, so instead I'll say how much I look forward to all the stories I *will* get to publish!

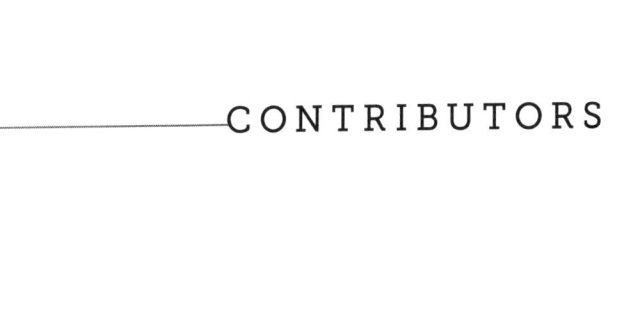

George Abraham is a Palestinian-American writer and Bioengineering Ph.D. candidate at Harvard. He is the author of *Birthright* (Button Poetry, 2020), and the chapbooks *the specimen's apology* (Sibling Rivalry Press, 2019) and *al youm* (TAR, 2017). Their work is forthcoming with *The Paris Review*, *Tin House*, *Literary Hub*, *Boston Review*, and elsewhere.

Reem Abu-Baker lives in Tuscaloosa, AL, where she teaches at the University of Alabama. Her writing has been published by *Mid-American Review*, *Ninth Letter*, and online at *Tin House*.

María Isabel Álvarez's writing has appeared in *Gulf Coast*, *Black Warrior Review*, *Sonora Review*, *Colorado Review*, and *The Rumpus*, among other venues, and has received support from the Arizona Commission on the Arts, the Tennessee Arts Commission, Sundress Academy for the Arts, and Hedgebrook.

Patriz Biliran graduated with honors from the University of the Philippines with a degree in Creative Writing. She is a published textbook author and currently works as a Content Specialist in an edtech startup company based in the Philippines.

Anna Cabe's work has appeared or is forthcoming in *Bitch*, *The Toast*, *SmokeLong Quarterly*, *Joyland*, and *Fairy Tale Review*, among others. She received her MFA in fiction from

CONTRIBUTORS

Indiana University and was formerly the nonfiction editor for *Indiana Review*. She is a 2018-2019 Fulbright Fellow in the Philippines. You can find Anna at annacabe.com.

Tyrese Coleman is an essayist, fiction writer, and the reviews editor for *SmokeLong Quarterly*. Her flash has appeared in several publications, including *PANK*, *Brevity*, *upstreet*, and elsewhere. A Kimbilio Fiction Fellow, her collection *How To Sit* is available from Mason Jar Press. Reach her at tyresecoleman.com or on Twitter @tylachelleco.

Allison Noelle Conner's writing has appeared in *Bitch*, *Full Stop*, *The Rumpus*, and elsewhere. Her essay on the short film *The Kitchen* by Alile Sharon Larkin and the fiction of Gayl Jones is included in the anthology *Rockhaven: A History of Interiors*. She lives in Los Angeles.

Desiree Cooper is a 2015 Kresge Artist Fellow, Pulitzer Prize-nominated journalist and author of the award-winning, debut collection of flash fiction *Know the Mother* (Wayne State University Press, 2016). "The Choice" is now a short film, available free online at descooper.com.

Erica Frederick is a Haitian-American writer from Orlando, Florida. She holds a bachelor's degree in Creative Writing from Florida State University and completed the Hurston/Wright Foundation Summer Writers Workshop in August of

2018. Her short fiction was a finalist in *Glimmer Train*.

Amina Gautier is the author of *At-Risk*, *Now We Will Be Happy*, and *The Loss of All Lost Things*. She has been awarded the Flannery O'Connor Award, the Prairie Schooner Book Prize, the International Latino Book Award, the Phillis Wheatley Award, and the PEN/Malamud Award for Excellence in the Short Story.

Marcos Gonsalez is an essayist living in New York City. His essay collection about growing up a gay son of an undocumented Mexican father and poor Puerto Rican mother in white America, *Pedro's Theory: Essays*, is represented by agent Lauren Abramo and currently on submission.

Christopher Gonzalez is a former Clevelander now living in New York. His short stories appear in *Third Point Press*, *Cosmonauts Avenue*, *JMWW*, and *Pithead Chapel*, among others. He serves as a fiction editor at *Barrelhouse* and contributing editor at *Split Lip*. Visit him online at chris-gonzalez.com or on Twitter @livesinpages.

Marlin M. Jenkins was born and raised in Detroit. His writings have found homes in *Indiana Review*, *Waxwing*, and *Iowa Review*. A teaching artist who works with youth in fiction and poetry, he also teaches writing and literature at University of Michigan, where he earned his MFA in poetry.

CONTRIBUTORS

Ruth Joffre is the author of the story collection *Night Beast* (Grove/Black Cat, 2018). Her work has appeared or is forthcoming in *Kenyon Review, The Masters Review, Lightspeed, Hayden's Ferry Review, Mid-American Review, Prairie Schooner, Nashville Review, Fiction Southeast*, and elsewhere.

Yalie Kamara is a Sierra Leonean-American writer and an Oakland native. She's the author of *A Brief Biography of My Name* (Akashic Books/APBF, 2018) and *When The Living Sing* (Ledge Mule Press, 2017). She is a doctoral student in Creative Writing and English Literature at the University of Cincinnati. yaylala.com

W. Todd Kaneko is the author of *The Dead Wrestler Elegies* (Curbside Splendor, 2014) and co-author of *Poetry: A Writer's Guide and Anthology* (Bloomsbury Academic, 2018). A Kundiman fellow, he is co-editor of *Waxwing*, and teaches creative writing at Grand Valley State University in Grand Rapids, Michigan.

Gene Kwak is from Omaha, Nebraska.

Kristine Ong Muslim is the author of nine books, most recently *The Drone Outside* (Eibonvale Press, 2017), and editor of two anthologies: the British Fantasy Award-winning *People of Colo(u)r Destroy Science Fiction* (with Nalo Hopkinson) and *Sigwa: Climate Fiction Anthology from the*

Philippines (with Paolo Enrico Melendez and Mia Tijam).

Thirii Myo Kyaw Myint is the author of the lyric novel *The End of Peril, the End of Enmity, the End of Strife, a Haven* (Noemi Press, 2018) and the family history project *Zat Lun*, which won the 2018 Graywolf Press Nonfiction Prize.

Monterica Sade Neil is a medium, a queer, Black creative, a Tin House Scholar, and third-year MFA candidate at Louisiana State University. She received her undergraduate degree in Creative Writing from The University of Tennessee at Chattanooga and is from Memphis, TN. She is currently at work on a memoir.

Dennis Norris II's writing appears in *The Rumpus*, *Apogee*, *SmokeLong Quarterly*, and elsewhere. They have been the recipient of fellowships from The MacDowell Colony, Tin House, and Kimbilio Fiction, and they co-host the popular podcast *Food 4 Thot*. You can find more information at dennisnorrisii.com.

Alvin Park lives and writes in Portland. He's associate fiction editor at *Little Fiction*. His work has been featured in *The Rumpus*, *The Mojave River Review*, *Wyvern Lit*, *Synaesthesia Magazine*, *Wildness*, and more. His parents are Korean. He has a long way to go.

CONTRIBUTORS

Madhvi Ramani writes articles, essays, drama and fiction. Her work has been published by *The New York Times*, *The Washington Post*, *Asia Literary Review*, and others. She was born in London and currently lives a thoroughly bohemian lifestyle in Berlin. Find out more at madhviramani.com or follow her on Twitter @madhviramani.

Alicita Rodríguez is a Cuban-American writer who lives in Denver. She loves impossible architectures, unusual animals, and fabulous tales.

Anuj Shrestha is a cartoonist and illustrator. His comics have been listed in several editions of *The Best American Comics* anthology. His illustration work has appeared in *The New York Times*, *The New Yorker*, *McSweeney's*, *Playboy*, and *Wired*, among others. He currently resides in Philadelphia, PA.

SJ Sindu is the award-winning author of the novel *Marriage of a Thousand Lies*, and the hybrid fiction and nonfiction chapbook, *I Once Met You But You Were Dead*. Sindu's work has appeared in numerous journals and anthologies. She was born in Sri Lanka and raised in Massachusetts.

Maggie Su is a fiction Ph.D. candidate at University of Cincinnati. Her work has appeared or is forthcoming in *DIAGRAM*, *Mid-American Review*, *Joyland*, *The Offing*, *The Journal*, *Green Mountains Review*, *SmokeLong Quarterly*, and elsewhere. She serves as a staff reader for *The Cincinnati Review* and *Ploughshares*.

Eshani Surya is an MFA student at the University of Arizona. Her writing has appeared in *Joyland*, *Literary Hub*, *Essay Daily*, and *Ninth Letter Online*, among others. She was the 2016 winner of *New Delta Review*'s Ryan R. Gibbs Award for Flash Fiction. Find her @__eshani or at eshani-surya.com.

Ursula Villarreal-Moura was born and raised in San Antonio, Texas. Her stories, essays, and reviews have appeared in *Catapult*, *Tin House* online, *Prairie Schooner*, *Bennington Review*, *Washington Square*, and *New South*. More at ursulavillarrealmoura.com.

Yun Wei received her MFA from Brooklyn College and a bachelor's in international relations from Georgetown University. Her fiction and poetry have appeared in *Wigleaf*, *Word Riot*, *Brooklyn Review*, and other journals. She currently works on global health development in Switzerland, where she consistently fails at mountain sports.

C. Pam Zhang's debut novel, *How Much of These Hills Is Gold*, is forthcoming from Riverhead Books in the US, as well as several international publishers. Her short fiction appears in *Kenyon Review*, *McSweeney's Quarterly*, and elsewhere. She's lived in thirteen cities and is still looking for home.

ACKNOWLEDGMENTS

"Here's the Situation" originally appeared in *JMWW*; "Collection" originally appeared in *Tin House* as "Gone Collecting;" "They Reminisce Over You" appeared in slightly different form in *Hobart*; "Yellow School Buses" originally appeared in *Vinyl Poetry and Prose*; "The Choice" originally appeared in *COG* as "First Response;" "Ghost Story" originally appeared in *Split Lip Magazine*; "Dobson Unit" originally appeared in *New South*; "Before" appeared in slightly different form in *Quarterly West*; "See Me" originally appeared in *Jellyfish Review*; "Between Colitis Flares, Expect the Following Symptoms" originally appeared in *New Delta Review*; "This House Is Our Burned Bodies" originally appeared in *Passages North*; "A Girl Turns to Stone" originally appeared in *The Offing*; "Peña Blanca, Guatemala" originally appeared in *Black Warrior Review*; "Mirror" originally appeared in *The Blueshift Journal*; "No Frills" appeared in slightly altered form in *Wigleaf*; "The Equivalent of ____" originally appeared in *WhiskeyPaper*; "Daddy's Boy" originally appeared in *SmokeLong Quarterly*; "Holocene: Microfilm Reel 82" originally appeared in *The Cincinnati Review*; "How to Catch a Sun" originally appeared in *Wigleaf*; and "Circumnavigation" originally appeared in *The Offing*.

DONORS

Forward was produced in association with Mythic Picnic (@mythicpicnic), and wouldn't have been possible without the enthusiasm and general contributions of Stephanie Bray, Mark Finnemore, Patrick Foran, Bix Gabriel, Jon Chaiim McConnell, Amy Rossi, and Marie Schutt. Thank you for helping us make this book!

ABOUT THE EDITOR

Megan Giddings is a fiction editor at *The Offing* and a contributing editor at *Boulevard*. Her debut novel, *Lakewood*, is forthcoming from Amistad in 2020. More about her can be found at megangiddings.com.

ABOUT THE PRESS

Aforementioned Productions is an award-winning small press and 501(c)(3) non-profit organization that publishes chapbooks, full-length collections of poetry and prose, and the weekly online/annual print literary journal *apt*; and produces theatrical performances and other literary events. Founded in 2005 and run by Carissa Halston and Randolph Pfaff, Aforementioned's aesthetic favors challenging writing that combines the cerebral and the visceral.

Aforementioned is supported primarily through book sales and reader contributions. Donations to Aforementioned are tax-deductible.

To make a donation, visit aforementioned.org/donate.